A DANGEROUS GAME

by

Geoff Collins

This book is a work of fiction. Names, characters, places and incidents are either the product of the author's imagination or are used fictitiously. Any resemblance to actual persons, living or dead, or to actual events or locales is entirely coincidental.

A DANGEROUS GAME

Front cover designed by: nskvsky at www.Fiverr.com
Front/Back cover art: nskvsky at www.Fiverr.com

Interior art: Silhouette of pitcher: Pixabay CC0 Creative Commons Free for commercial use
Interior art: Dog illustration: Pixabay CC0 Creative Commons Free for commercial use

Edited by Joe Gartrell and Ben Gibson of Word Mule. www.wordmule.com

Published by A&J Publishing, LLC
3266 Hartwell Street
Johns Island, SC 29455

Visit the author's website: www.booksbycollins.com

Categories: FICTION / Thrillers / Crime

ISBN: 978-1-951744-57-1 (ebook)
ISBN: 978-1-951744-58-8 (paperback)

Version: 2021.03.05

www.projectpawsalive.org

A special thanks to Joe Gartrell and Ben Gibson of Word Mule.
www.wordmule.com

This book is dedicated to …

Arthur and Irene Collins

BOOKS BY GEOFF COLLINS

★★★★★

"A Holy City Mystery Artfully Spun"

"Geoff Collins is a wonderfully versatile writer (check out his bibliography), and here, he weaves a delightful mystery set in the Holy City. Hop along and crack this case with Giordano—you won't regret, and it will get you primed for the other books coming along in the series."

★★★★★

"Well Written … Interesting Characters and Plenty of Suspense"

"Good mystery with interesting characters and plenty of suspense. A cybersecurity expert is hired to determine if narcotics theft is taking place at Charleston SC hospital and who is behind it. Well written with lots of fascinating details."

"Wonderfully Crafted Story Set in Charleston"

"Wonderfully crafted story set in Charleston, SC—great story line and vivid imagery. Collins follows Giordano with insight and honesty. Can't wait for Nick's next adventure."

"A Fast and Exciting Read"

"The book was a fast read. It was exciting and held my interest throughout. Hope to see more from this author."

"Another Wild Ride"

*"*Tools of the Trade *takes us on another wild ride with Nick Giordano and his crew. Collins, as he did with his previous book in this three-part series, deftly weaves on intricate story line that builds to a satisfying, thrilling end. Highly recommend Collins, a writer who deserves a vast readership."*

"Excitement and Suspense"

"Excitement and suspense as mafia and white supremacists fight over the drug market in Charleston SC. Characters well-developed and interesting story line."

"Hopefully More to Come"

"In this series, which sadly wraps here with Book Three, Collins found a higher gear with each, serving up a fresh batch of nasty folks for the series' core characters to root out and take down. That the books were set in Charleston only added to their delight. The only rotten aspect here is that this is the last we'll see of Nick Giordano and his pals—that is, unless, this crew comes around for cameos in one of Collins' future works. Hats off!"

"Baseball is ninety percent mental, and the other half is physical."
—Yogi Berra

"When the Fox hears the Rabbit scream, he come a-runnin', but not to help."
—Thomas Harris, *The Silence of the Lambs*

A Dangerous Game

PROLOGUE

IT WAS APPROACHING ten Monday night as a dark blanket of fog rolled off the ocean and descended on downtown Norfolk, bringing with it the promise of rain. Harbor Park Stadium was almost empty, the last lines of cars and trucks snaking their way from the parking lot.

Joe Nash bent down, untied his spikes, and slid them into his locker. He remained hunched over, massaging his left elbow. He'd pitched two and a third innings of middle relief that night, giving up four hits, two walks, and three earned runs before he was pulled in the bottom of the eighth. It was yet another in a string of ineffective outings for Joe. He started unbuttoning his jersey when he heard a quiet voice. "Joe, Skipper wants to see you in his office."

Joe glanced back and saw Luis Garcia, the Tides' first base coach.

"Thanks, Coach." He waited until Garcia was out of earshot and then muttered to himself. "Shit."

This was Joe's fifth year in the Orioles' minor league system, his second year at Triple-A. It was also by far his worst. He'd been a productive starter his entire career. But a 6.30 ERA this year had cost him his place in the starting rotation and relegated him to middle relief. He was slowly coming to accept that his lifelong dream was falling apart on the doorstep of the major leagues.

He made his way from the locker room and down the hall to Manager John Mercer's office. A few teammates glanced his way as he was leaving the locker room but said nothing. They'd all witnessed this scene play out before. It's either good news or bad news—you're either moving up or getting sent down.

The door was open, Mercer seated behind his desk. Pete Rollins, the Tides' pitching coach, was also in the room. Joe stuck his head in. "Skipper, you wanted to see me?"

"Yeah, Joe, come on in." Mercer turned to Rollins. "We'll talk about that later."

As he was leaving, Rollins patted Joe on the back but said nothing.

"Shut the door and have a seat, Joe."

Mercer's small office was filled with memorabilia from his four years as a utility infielder with the Mets and Red Sox and his twenty-plus years coaching in the minor leagues. Mercer was in his late fifties, the lines in his face a roadmap of his journey. He'd had two short coaching stints in the majors with San

Diego and Philadelphia but preferred the minors where he could use his knowledge of the game to groom younger players.

"How's the arm, Joe?"

"A little sore, but it'll be all right."

Mercer was quiet for a moment—his look somber and severe. "Your velocity's down, and your mechanics are off. Coach Rollins is convinced it's because of your elbow problems, and I tend to agree with him."

Joe was quiet. He knew Rollins was right, but before he could craft a defense, Mercer continued, "We're going to make some moves. I got a call from Baltimore this morning. Two Double-A pitchers are being moved up here from Hagerstown, and I've got to make room for them. We're putting you on the IR list because of your elbow." Mercer passed a slip of paper across his desk. "That's the phone number for Dr. Sidney Wallace at Johns Hopkins. He's expecting you in Baltimore Wednesday. He'll arrange for an MRI and some other tests."

"How long will I be on IR?" There was less than a month left in the season. Joe knew if he lost his spot on the team, it would be tough getting it back.

"Right now, it's a 20-day," Mercer answered. "We may reassess when we get the results from Wallace."

"Hell, John, the season will almost be over by the time I get off IR."

"Let's just wait and see what the doctor comes up with," Mercer said. "The alternative is to option you down to Hagerstown. Management hasn't given up on you, and neither have I. Let the doctors do what they do, and we'll deal with the situation based on what they find." Mercer stood—the meeting was over. "That's the way it's going to be, Joe. Now get some ice on that arm."

CHAPTER 1

JOE SPENT THIRTY minutes in the trainer's room dealing with the pain in his left elbow and a growing anxiety about his future. He'd been relatively free of serious injuries throughout his career—incredibly unusual for a pitcher. But his luck ran out during spring training when he began to feel a twinge of discomfort in his left elbow. The problem slowly worsened as the season progressed, as did his performance.

By the time he got back to the locker room, the few remaining players had figured Joe was gone and kept their distance. They all knew the drill.

Joe dressed without showering and made his way to the stadium parking lot. The sky was overcast, the air swollen with moisture. A light drizzle had begun to fall, and the lot was virtually deserted as he got into his 2015 Ford Ranger. He sat there for a time, wondering about his future in the game he loved so dearly. The meeting with Mercer had left him emotionally spent, and he knew sleep would be out of the question.

Rather than heading to his studio apartment in Chesterfield Heights, he decided to stop at Brother's Bar and Grill—the team's favorite watering hole.

~~~~

It was after eleven by the time he got to the bar, and the place was dead. Its eight widescreens were tuned to an assortment of golf, ESPN, and West Coast baseball.

Joe grabbed a barstool and nodded at the bartender. "Hey, Jerry. How about an IPA draft and a shot of Jack?"

"You want a shot?" Joe had been coming into Brother's for the past two years, and the bartender had never seen him drink more than a few beers.

"That's what I said."

"All right. You got it." The bartender gave Joe his beer and shot.

Joe took a pull of his beer, downed the shot of Jack, and tried to come to terms with the last five years of his life. He was almost twenty-eight, and he knew that there was no guarantee that surgery, should he need it, would be successful. Surgery would also require a year or two of intense rehab to fully re-cover, putting another significant dent in any hope of making it to "the Show."

The beers and shots began to add up, and soon he felt a wave of nostalgia wash over him. Baseball had been the bed-rock of his life. Some of his earliest memories were of playing catch with his father in the backyard of their small home in Mt.
~~~~

Pleasant, South Carolina. Even at a young age, little Joe displayed an advanced proficiency for the game, and at the tender age of seven, Joe's dad made a decision—his son would be a pitcher. Frank Nash excelled in high school ball but was never more than average at the college level. Despite that, he considered himself a "student of the game." He knew left-handed pitchers who throw hard and can find the plate are among the most valued players in baseball.

Frank prodded and pushed his son relentlessly. Every weekend and many weekday evenings, he would spend hours working with Joe, teaching him the finer aspects of pitching. He even built a pitcher's mound in his backyard, and soon little Joe was developing a variety of pitches. Frank was hard on his son. But there was on occasion a sweetness, too. He could sense when Joe was growing weary and would try to restore him with a gift of a package of *Topps* or *Upper Deck* baseball cards. Over the years, Joe's collection became impressive—containing several sought-after cards like Barry Bonds' 1984 rookie card and a 1979 card signed by Tom Seaver. The Nash family was far from rich, but Frank would scrape up enough money to send Joe to the most elite baseball camps in the South every summer.

As a freshman at Wando High School, Joe was already six foot and a solid 175, looking more like a senior. It didn't take long for him to secure his place in the starting rotation. He ended that year winning seven games and losing only twice. And he just kept getting better, finishing his sophomore year with a 1.25 ERA and a conference-leading 102 strikeouts.

Frank never missed a game. He was quick with praise when Joe excelled, but he didn't hesitate to berate him in front of his peers when his performance didn't meet his expectations.

Wando baseball had long been a force and was consistently in the mix for the "AAAA" State Championship. Joe's ERA dropped, and his strikeouts increased during his junior year, and soon a stream of college scouts began showing up at his games. By the beginning of his senior year, he'd already received over twenty scholarship offers—many from elite schools like Arizona State, Clemson, Miami, and Florida State.

February 1, 2011, was a big day for Joe—National Signing Day when senior athletes announce what college they plan to attend in the fall. Joe, his mother, father, and sister, along with his high school coach, were all at the high school to participate in the event, which was covered by local television stations. Joe and Frank had narrowed the field to three: Arizona State, Oklahoma, and Clemson. It wasn't until the morning of the signing that the decision was finally made. It would be Arizona State. Joe leaned toward Clemson, closest to home, but his dad pressured him to choose Arizona State because it consistently drafted more major league pitchers than any other school.

The excitement continued throughout the week until Sunday, when Frank and his mom, Ruth, sat him down for a talk.

"Your mother and I received some news this past Monday," Frank began. "And the news is not good." He turned toward Ruth and nodded for her to continue.

She was obviously nervous and had to look away from Joe before she could begin. "I saw Dr. Morrison early last week for my annual checkup, and the mammogram showed a problem in my left breast. I had a biopsy taken, and the results showed Stage 2 breast cancer. That's the bad news, but the good news is that the tumor is small, and the doctors think they caught it relatively early—so my prognosis is good. I'm going to need surgery and then some follow-up radiation and chemotherapy, but Dr. Morrison says I should be okay after that."

"Son, your mother is tough," Frank broke in. "She's going to be just fine. We know you've worked hard, and you've got a great opportunity next year at Arizona State. We don't want you to worry about this thing."

This thing. Joe recoiled at the words. He was quiet for a time, trying to process what he'd just heard. Aside from colds and the occasional flu, no one in the family had ever been really sick, but he realized how severe the disease could be if not caught early.

Finally, he got up, kissed his mom on the cheek, and whispered, "I love you, Mom. We're going to be okay."

Frank stood and clapped his hands. "Come on, Son. Mom needs to talk to Emily. Let's work on that knuckle curve."

Instead of following him out, Joe returned to his seat. "Dad, we're not done here."

Half confused, half perturbed, Frank turned back and asked, "So, what do you want, Son?"

"Sit down, Dad."

Frank frowned and reluctantly sat.

"I'm not a child anymore," Joe continued. "I know what Stage 2 cancer means." He turned to his mom. "Has the cancer spread to your lymph nodes?"

"No, Joe," Ruth said, "they don't think so."

"Good," he said and turned back to face his dad. "First off, there's no way I'm going anywhere while Mom's having those treatments. The College of Charleston offered me a full scholarship. Plus, I really liked Coach Lee, and Charleston made it to the semifinals in the College World Series last year."

Frank shot a disgusted look at his wife. "Hold on, Son. We've already signed that Letter of Intent for Arizona State. We need to stick with the plan."

Joe stood. "No, Dad. The plan just changed. I'm playing for Coach Lee. That's my decision." He switched his attention back to his mother. "Mom, let's go talk to Emily. I want to be with you when you tell her."

Frank's face had turned a bright red. He wasn't used to his decisions being questioned, especially by his son. "Damn it, Son. We're talking about your future here!"

"No, Dad," Joe shot back. "We're talking about Mom's future! I'm staying, and that's the way it's going to be. Get used to it. Come on, Mom. Let's find Emily."

~~~~

Joe's decision to stay in Charleston marked a turning point in his relationship with his father. He no longer worked out with
~~~~

his dad but instead began spending more time with his team-mates. While Joe drifted away from his father, a chasm began growing between Frank and the rest of the family.

The week after sharing the grim news with her kids, Ruth underwent a lumpectomy to remove the tumor. Joe and Emily were with Ruth during her outpatient surgery—Frank didn't show up until she was being checked out. He said he got "tied up at the office." He was a CPA with his own small accounting and investment business, and for the next few weeks, he began spending more and more time there—sometimes not getting home until late into the night.

The radiation and chemotherapy following the surgery hit Ruth hard, and with Frank gone most of the time, Joe and Emily pretty much ran the household.

Ruth completed her chemo by summer's end, and things began to look up as her health slowly improved. Joe remained busy training with a small group of local College of Charleston recruits, and Emily enjoyed playing with her friends in the neighborhood or hanging with a host of fellow computer geeks online. Apart from his father, things were returning to normal. Frank's emotional and physical drift continued, and he was rarely at home anymore.

In late August, Joe moved into a dorm and began pre-season practices with Coach Lee and the team. His roommate, Alex Cooper, was an All-State catcher from Atlanta. The two immediately hit it off and grew to be close friends.

Joe picked up where he left off on the baseball field, quickly working his way into the Cougars' starting rotation.

Despite the school's rigorous academic demands and a packed baseball schedule, he always managed to spend time at home with his mom and sister. By early autumn, Ruth's doctor okayed her return to her third-grade classroom and the profession that she loved so much.

That year, Joe's 11 wins and just 3 losses helped Charleston make it all the way to the NCAA Regional finals. By the end of his first year of college, he was convinced his decision to attend the College of Charleston was the right one. He finished the school year with a solid 3.2 GPA and had developed a good group of friends—both on and off the baseball field. He allowed himself a bit of quiet satisfaction when he learned the Arizona State Sun Devils finished their season with a disappointing 24 and 16 and were eliminated during the first-round of their conference playoffs.

~~~~

Joe's success at school stood in stark contrast with his further disintegrating relationship with his father, who had taken to spending days-long stretches away from home. He always blamed work, claiming to have taken on a highly demanding new client, but Emily told Joe that even when he was home, he was off by himself somewhere. That summer, Joe, Alex, and a few other players rented a small house downtown. Joe split his time between daily workouts with his teammates, bussing tables at High Cotton, and spending as much time as possible at home in Mt. Pleasant.
~~~~

The inevitable finally came in August—Frank said he wanted a divorce. He'd been having an affair with his secretary and announced he would move in with her. While not entirely unexpected, this was devastating for Ruth. Despite his absence, she'd held out hope that Frank would eventually make amends and recommit to her and the family. The next month or two was brutal as the lawyers worked their way through the process. It cost a small fortune—when all was said and done, there wasn't much left. Ruth ended up with the house and half their money. Frank agreed to monthly child support payments for Emily and arranged for a small fund to be set up for her college education.

Joe was furious with his father and refused to have anything to do with him after the divorce. The split also affected his performance on the field. He lost three of his first six starts his sophomore year. However, things slowly evolved into a new normal as the situation's finality settled in. Emily excelled academically in middle school, Ruth found some comfort with her teaching career, and Joe settled back into college life—spending whatever free time he had with his mom and sister.

Joe recovered from his early losses, winning his last six starts and ending the season with a respectable 9 and 3 record. The Cougars again made it to the semifinals before losing their final game in extra innings to Clemson.

Like the previous summer, Alex and Joe rented an apartment downtown and continued playing ball, working, and enjoying summer in the Lowcountry. But in early July, Joe's world came crashing down when he learned his mom's cancer had returned. It had metastasized—spreading to other parts of her body. Joe moved out of his apartment and spent the rest of the summer at home in Mt. Pleasant.

Ruth's condition worsened as the summer progressed, and rather than returning for his junior year, Joe decided to drop out of school to stay home and help care for his mom. It was no surprise that he heard little from his father during this time as he remained estranged from the family.

As the months passed, the cancer returned with a vengeance, spreading quickly to her lungs, bones, and brain. Ruth fought hard through another bout of chemo, but it soon became apparent she was losing the battle. In late November, she entered hospice, where she remained until she died a week before Christmas. Joe and Emily were by her side when she passed. She was buried five days later, with Joe taking care of the church service and funeral arrangements.

The weather was unseasonably warm, and the sky overcast the day of the funeral. The scent of rain was in the air as people gathered for Ruth's service. The church was filled to capacity— a testament to the life she led and the many people she had touched. The service was heartwarming, with Ruth's pastor talking about how loving and caring a life she led. Frank was at the service, but he sat in the back and left immediately after.

A small group of close family friends joined Joe and Emily at the cemetery. Joe said a few heartfelt words at the gravesite, conveying what a wonderful mother she had been and the courage she displayed during her fight with cancer. The ceremony ended with Joe and Emily placing white roses on Ruth's casket and offering their final goodbyes before their mother was lowered into the ground.

Joe and Emily were walking back to the car hand in hand when Frank approached and said, "Son, can we talk?"

"Em, go on ahead." He then turned to face his father. "So you want to talk? After walking out on your wife and family? No, Dad, I don't think so. You can go straight to hell as far as I'm concerned." Joe turned and walked off without saying another word.

CHAPTER 2

JOE RETURNED TO college in early January. He found it somewhat cathartic when he learned Frank's affair with his secretary lasted less than six months. She left him, quit the company, and moved home to Nashville. After the breakup, Frank bought a small house in Mt. Pleasant. Ruth's house was sold, and after paying off the remaining mortgage and debts Ruth had incurred, there wasn't much left for Joe and Emily. It was Emily's first year in high school, and sadly, she had no choice but to move in with her father.

Joe ended his junior season with a 13 and 3 record and helped carry his team to the World Series championship game. The Cougars fought hard but were edged out by Florida State. A few days after the team returned to Charleston, Coach Lee called Joe into his office.

"You had a hell of a season, Joe."

"Thanks, Coach." Then a mischievous smile appeared on Coach Lee's face, the smirk twisting as he watched Joe's curiosity pique. Joe returned the smile. "What?"

"Apparently, I wasn't the only one impressed with your season. I've received a few calls from major league scouts interested in drafting you."

"Seriously?" Joe's excitement was palpable. "Which teams?"

"Baltimore is a lock, and Boston, Miami, and Houston are serious, too. I'll know in the next day or so."

"I figured I'd get drafted—just didn't know what teams would be interested. Are they talking with anyone else on the team?"

"A few are interested in Cooper and Jeffries," Coach answered.

"That's great! What do I do?"

One of the perks of being a coach was watching your players' dedication and hard work pay off. "They'll be here in my office on Friday. If you're not too busy ..."

"Are you kidding me?" Joe was on his feet now. "Hell yes, I'll be here!"

Joe showed up at Coach Lee's office a few minutes before noon on Friday. Coach told him to come in and have a seat. Joe caught a sly smile on Lee's face and asked, "Which teams am I going to see, Coach?"

"Baltimore and Boston," Coach said and spent a few minutes giving Joe some tips on what to say and how to handle the interviews. "These teams are here to gauge your interest and willingness to play ball for them before they pull the trigger to choose you in the upcoming draft. They'll probably drop some hints about possible signing bonuses. Listen to what they have to say, but don't make any commitments."

The interviews went well, with Baltimore and Boston accentually promising Joe a spot on their rookie league squad. Baltimore dropped a figure of a probable $45,000 signing bonus—Boston's was a bit lower at $40,500. Joe was thrilled with the prospect of becoming a professional ballplayer—a goal he'd worked so hard to obtain. His excitement was tempered by the paltry amount of the signing bonuses. He also was well aware that the minor league salary for first-year players was only $400 a week and $35 per diem for travel expenses.

Ruth's estate didn't amount to much, so money would be a significant problem if he were drafted with such a small signing bonus. The other issue was that if he accepted a draft offer, he would have to quit school and forego his senior year. The situation was confounded by the fact that Frank had been given full custody of Emily after Ruth's death. Emily would have to continue living with Frank throughout her junior and senior years in high school. Joe clearly did not trust his father. He sought Coach Lee's guidance, and after weighing the pros and cons of being drafted, Joe decided to return for his senior year. Coach believed that if he performed well in his final year, his value would undoubtedly increase, and he'd have a shot at moving up in next year's MLB draft.

Joe's decision turned out to be the right one. He finished his final season at Charleston with a solid 12 and 2 record and another strong finish in the NCAA playoffs. On the first day of the 2015 MLB draft, Joe and several of his fellow players got together at Coach Lee's house to watch. Three Cougars were drafted that year, with Joe going to the Baltimore Orioles in the sixth round and at $100,000, his signing bonus had more than doubled.

On a Saturday toward the middle of May, with giant live oaks draped in Spanish moss as a backdrop, Joe strode across the ceremonial stage at the College of Charleston to receive his diploma. With the degree in hand, he paused and pointed up to a clear summer sky and whispered, "This is for you, Mom."

Bright and early the following morning, Joe left in his brand new Ford Ranger on a 2,100 mile trip to Phoenix and the start of his professional baseball career.

CHAPTER 3

IT WAS 1:30 in the morning, and Joe was the only customer still at Brother's. The Dodgers and Cubs game was on the widescreen behind the bar, but Joe was having a hard time focusing on the TV. He'd lost track of the shots and beers he'd consumed over the last two and a half hours as he mused over the highs and lows of his life.

He started flexing his left elbow. What the hell was he going to do. Baseball had always been there for him—through the good times and bad. He was so close to his dream; he could almost taste it. But now, he could feel it slipping away.

"Joe! I said we're closing up."

Joe was brought back to reality when the bartender appeared in front of him. Joe squinted and slurred, "Hey, there, Berry. What's up? Did you know I struck out Aaron Judge and Giancarlo Stanton the first time I faced them in spring training?" Joe laughed. "They both homered the next time I pitched to them. How about one more beer for the road and get one for yourself."

"No, Joe. I'm good, and it's Jerry, not Berry. I just called you a cab. No way are you driving home tonight."

"Sure. Whatever you say, buddy." Joe pulled out a handful of bills and put them on the bar. "How much do I owe you?"

Jerry took enough to cover his bar tab plus a healthy tip and slid the rest back to Joe. "Sit tight. I'll let you know when your ride gets here."

Joe smiled and gave an exaggerated salute. His eyes turned back to the game on the TV. A few minutes later, the lights came on in the bar, and the cab arrived. Joe barely remembered the ride to his apartment.

~~~~

There was a ringing sound in his ear. It continued until he realized it was his cell phone. He reached over to pick it up but knocked it off the nightstand. "Shit."

Rolling to the side of the bed, he reached down and felt around until he found the phone. Lifting it, he managed a weak, "Hello?"

"I've been trying to get ahold of you for the last hour!" Emily said. She was clearly agitated. "Where are you?"

Joe reluctantly opened his eyes and saw the window shades were wide open. The bright morning sun was streaming in—forcing him to quickly shut his eyes. His head felt like it had been hit with a baseball bat. "Hey, Em."
~~~~

"Where are you?"

Joe opened an eye. He still had on the same clothes he'd worn the night before—then he remembered the bar and the shots and beers. "In my apartment. What's up?"

"It's Dad!"

"What about him?"

"He's dead! Joe, Dad's dead!"

Joe sat bolt upright, his head spinning. "Wait a minute. He's dead? What happened?"

"I don't know," Emily answered. "I got a call about an hour ago from a detective named Max Decker. He told me Michelle went to check on him after he didn't show up for work yesterday. She had a key to the house and found him about 9:30 this morning slumped over a chair in the living room. He wasn't breathing, and she called 9-1-1."

"Wait a minute. Who's Michelle?"

"She's Dad's secretary."

"Shit, let me think," Joe said. It didn't seem real to him. "Do they know what happened?"

"Joe, I just told you everything I know! Listen to me. Dad's dead! The coroner's at his house now. That's all I know."

"Where are you now?" Joe asked.

"My apartment. Decker wants to talk with me downtown at the police station later today. I'll know more then."

Joe glanced at his cell and saw it was almost eleven. "All right, I need to make a few calls. I'll leave as soon as I clean up and should get there between seven and eight. Call me as soon as you finish at the police station, and we'll decide what to do."

A hot shower, four aspirin, and two cups of black coffee helped clear some of the cobwebs and allowed the reality of his father's death to hit home. His dad was dead, and even though he hadn't spoken a word to him in over five years, a sense of loss began to settle over him—a profound sadness that comes when a person realizes both parents are gone. With it comes an understanding that you are now truly alone in the world. The pain and disappointment Joe felt toward his dad were, at least for the moment, overshadowed by childhood memories of a father he'd once loved and respected.

He threw some clothes in his backpack and was about to leave when he realized he'd left his car at Brother's. An Uber dropped him off at the bar, and he was on the road shortly after noon. He'd been driving for about an hour when Emily called.

"Did you talk to that detective yet?" Joe asked.

"No, but his partner told me they think it might have been a heart attack. I told him you'd be here later tonight. They want to talk to you first thing in the morning."

"I can't believe it was a heart attack. Hell, Dad was only in his early fifties. He never had any health problems. He may have been an ass, but he was definitely a healthy one."

"Decker said I need to go to the morgue this afternoon to formally identify Dad before they do an autopsy. God, I can't believe he's dead."

"I know, Em. I wish I were there to help."

"That's okay. I can handle it. Is there anything else I should be doing?"

"Let me think," Joe said. "Did the detective say how long Dad had been dead before the secretary found him?"

"I don't know. I never asked."

"Hell, for all we know, it might have been days," Joe said. "It's probably the first time he's missed work in decades."

"God, Joe," Emily said. "None of this makes sense."

"I know. I'll meet the detective in the morning and see what he says."

"All right. I'm sorry, Joe. I completely spaced out the last time we talked. You can obviously stay with Cindy and me at the duplex."

"Thanks, Sis, but I already called Alex Cooper. I'm going to stay with him at his place on Bull Street."

"That's only a few minutes from me. Call me right before you get in, and I can meet you there."

"Sounds good. And let me know if you learn anything new."

Joe continued his drive south out of Virginia following I-95 through North Carolina and into South Carolina—arriving in Charleston at 8:30 Tuesday evening.

~~~~

Alex Cooper received an offer from the Boston Red Sox after his junior year, but like Joe, he decided to stay in school. Unfortunately, midway through his final season, a horrific collision at home plate ruptured his Achilles. Being a catcher, an
~~~~

injury like that put an end to any hope of a professional baseball career. However, he remained in school earning his MBA and was now enjoying a lucrative career as an associate in J.P. Morgan's Wealth Management Division.

He was waiting when Joe pulled up in front of his house. "Joe Nash! How's the CY Young contender?" Alex asked.

"Not so good, buddy. Listen, I really appreciate you letting me crash at your place for a few days."

"No problem," Alex quickly replied. "I'm sorry about your dad. Any news about what happened?"

Joe passed on what little he knew, including where and when his dad was found. The tone of his voice made it clear that he questioned the police's initial opinion that his dad's death was most likely the result of a heart attack.

"I get the feeling you're not buying the heart attack thing," Alex said.

"No, not really. Emily said there'd be an autopsy, so we should know more after that."

"Just let me know what I can do to help," Alex offered.

"Thanks, I appreciate that."

Joe grabbed his backpack and followed Alex inside. The newly renovated two-bedroom, two-bath house was small but definitely upscale. Joe looked around the spacious living room, taking in the expensive furnishings. He couldn't help but compare it to the small studio he'd lived in the past two years. It reminded him how difficult it had become to live on his minor league salary.

Feeling a bit awkward and seeking a little conversational normalcy, Joe said, "Looks like someone's moving up in the world."

"I don't know about that," Alex answered with a smile. "But I have to admit things have been good in the market lately. What about you? How's it going with Baltimore?"

"That's another story," Joe answered. "We can talk about that later."

Alex was about to say something when his cell rang. He checked the number and said, "Sorry, Joe. It's my boss. I need to take this one."

Alex left for the bedroom and some privacy when there was a knock on the door. "That's probably Emily," Joe called after him. "I'll get it."

Joe let her in, and after a long hug, he noticed her eyes were red. She'd been crying. "How are you holding up, Sis?"

"I'll be okay," Emily said. "Where's Alex?"

"He's on a call with his boss. Come on in and sit down. Are you sure you're all right?"

"Not really," she answered. "I was at the coroner's office this afternoon. God, Joe, Dad looked absolutely terrible. His face was all shrunken. He didn't even look like Dad."

"I'm sorry you had to do that. Did you learn anything else from that detective?"

"It was really strange. I kept asking him and the coroner about Dad. They both kept saying they'd know more after the autopsy. I felt like they were hiding something. Decker asked a lot of questions but didn't give me many answers."

"What did he want to know?" Joe asked.

"He asked where Dad worked and if he was living with anyone. I told him Mom died a few years ago, and I didn't think he was involved with anyone. He wanted to know about his health and if he had any heart problems. I told him he was healthy as far as I knew. Then he asked if he had any enemies—God, Joe, it was just like in the movies. I told him I didn't know one way or the other. You know I rarely see him anymore. He calls every once in a while, asking if I need money or anything. I haven't taken a penny from him since high school."

"I know what you mean," Joe said. "I haven't said a word to him since Mom's funeral."

"There was one thing now that I think of it," Emily said. "Dad called me about a week or so ago and asked if I could have dinner with him. He said he had something important to tell me, but I had a big paper due and sort of blew him off. The strangest thing is that before he hung up, he said he loved me and missed me. He sounded all emotional. That's not Dad. What do you suppose that was all about?"

Before Joe could answer, Alex returned from his call.

"Hey, Emily. It's nice to see you again. I wish it were under better circumstances. Can I get you guys something to drink? I've got Voodoo Ranger IPA or good old Budweiser."

"Do you have a ginger ale or Coke?" Joe asked. "I had a few too many beers last night."

Alex smiled. "Hey, that happens to the best of us. I'll get you a Coke. How about you, Emily?"

"IPA sounds good," she said. "Thanks, Alex."

"You got it," he replied. He returned with the drinks and said, "So, Joe, we're in September—what are the chances the Orioles will call you up when they expand their roster? God knows you've paid your dues."

"I'm not sure that's going to happen this year," Joe had to admit. He went on to explain his arm problems and the 20-day injured reserve list. "I'm supposed to see the doctors in Baltimore on Wednesday. Obviously, that's not going to happen. To tell you the truth, I'm not sure what I'm going to do."

"Wait a second!" Emily interrupted. "You didn't tell me you got hurt."

"I only found out about the IR thing yesterday. To be honest, I'm not all that concerned about it now—we've got Dad to deal with."

"That sucks, buddy," Alex said. "You were the best damn pitcher I ever caught. I know you can still make it. These doctors can do amazing things nowadays."

"Thanks, Alex. We'll see what happens. But for now, I'm beat and need to hit the sack. I didn't sleep too well last night."

"No problem. I've got the back bedroom set up for you. I'm out of here first thing in the morning, but there's coffee on the counter and plenty of food in the fridge. I put an extra key on the table by the front door. Oh, and let's plan to meet tomorrow for lunch at the Old Town Grill."

"Thanks and lunch sounds good. Come on, Em, I'll walk you back."

"You don't need to do that," Emily protested. "I'm a big girl now."

"I know you are, but you're still my little sister," Joe said with a smile.

Walking back to Alex's house after dropping off Emily, Joe couldn't get over how grown-up she seemed. She was a shy and somewhat awkward sixteen-year-old when Joe left Charleston for Arizona. He'd played winter ball in Puerto Rico during the off-seasons and rarely made it back to Charleston. But now, that awkward sixteen-year-old had shed her chrysalis and emerged as a mature and confident young woman.

After Joe dropped Emily off at her place, he took his time walking back to Alex's house. The night was calm and clear, and his thoughts wandered back to his dad and the games of catch they'd played before he turned his back on the family. He remembered the first time his dad taught him how to throw a curveball. He felt a pang of pain in his elbow with the thought.

He slept soundly that night—dreaming he was young again, playing catch with his dad under the warmth of a clear, deep-blue summer sky.

CHAPTER 4

JOE CHECKED IN with the desk sergeant at the Lockwood police station the following morning and was told someone would be with him shortly. The remnants of the shots and beer had passed, and his mind was clear. There was a lot to be done—the funeral arrangements, dealing with his dad's estate, and the situation with the Orioles. And what about his dad's business? He was trying to remember the name of his dad's secretary when he heard a guttural, "Mr. Nash, I'm Detective Max Decker, and this is Detective Justin Glass."

Joe looked up and saw a short, somber-looking man in khaki pants and a navy blue polo carrying the Charleston Police Department's insignia. He had a shaved head and skin the color of dark-brown ebony. It wasn't easy to gauge his age, but lines spider-webbed around his eyes and mouth—the late forties or early fifties, Joe surmised. A curt, "Come with me," gave Joe the sense the guy was all business. His partner, Detective Justin

Glass, was white and looked to be much younger—around thirty. He wore a light brown suit—his shirt collar loosened, and tie yanked down. He was well over six feet and probably weighed north of 220. Although the difference in size and stature, Glass seemed comfortable standing behind Decker, deferring to his partner with an occasional nod. It was clear Glass played second fiddle to Decker.

Joe followed them down a hall into an open area divided into several semiprivate workspaces by a series of gray-colored steel panels. Each workspace was large enough to house desks and filing cabinets for two detectives. Glass took a seat behind one of the desks. Decker pointed to a chair next to his desk and said, "Sit." Joe sat, and the detective continued. "First off, I'm sorry for your loss. I got some of what I needed from your sister yesterday and just have a few questions for you."

"Certainly," Joe responded, feeling as though he'd done something wrong and was about to get interrogated. *Hell*, he thought, *I'm the one with questions!*

"Your sister told me she hadn't spent much time with your father," Decker stated. "I'm just wondering about your relationship with him."

"Not good, I'm afraid. I've spent very little time in Charleston over the last five years, and to be honest, I haven't had any contact with him."

Decker was disappointed. "What about the last few weeks? Any contact with him at all?"

"No. Sorry, but like I just said, I haven't had any involvement with him. But I do have some questions for you. You told my sister my dad died of a heart attack. Are you sure that was the case?"

Decker ignored the question. "What can you tell me about his company, Nash and Associates?"

"Well, associates might be a little bit misleading. I understand it was just my dad and his secretary."

"What can you tell me about her?" asked Decker.

"Detective, I never even met her. I've told you several times I haven't seen or talked to my father in years."

"It's my understanding that you and your sister are the only living relatives. Is that true?"

"Yes, it's only the two of us. Why do you ask?"

"Just tying up a few loose ends. That's all."

"Wait a minute, detective. If my dad died of a heart attack, why all the questions?" He was growing even more leery of the detective.

After a few more general questions about Joe's father, Decker said, "I think that's all for now," Decker said and stood. "Detective Glass will walk you out."

Joe remained seated. "My sister told me there'd be an autopsy. Has that been done, and If so, when can we see the results?"

"I expect I'll be getting a call from the coroner today."

"And when can we see the results?" Joe asked again.

"I'll need to talk to the coroner before anything is released," Decker said and glanced at his watch. "Thank you for coming in this morning, and I'll let you know if we need anything else from you or your sister. Now, I'm sure you have a busy day in front of you, and so do we."

Joe couldn't understand the detective's condescending attitude, and he wasn't about to put up with it. "Listen, Detective Decker, I came in here to help you and learn about my father's death. Now I'm getting the feeling there are some things you're not telling me."

Decker nodded to his partner, and Glass said, "If you'll come with me, sir?"

Joe had had enough. He stood and said, "I suppose I'll need to find some answers myself."

Joe turned to leave when Decker said, "Do you know anything about the gun we found in your father's kitchen?"

Joe stopped dead in his tracks. His dad would never think of ever having a gun in his house. Joe turned around. "No. He never owned a gun as far as I know."

"Well, we found one. A Glock G42. It was purchased about a month ago from the Limehouse Gun Shop on Johns Island and registered to your father. I'm just wondering why he would decide to buy one."

"I have no idea, detective," Joe answered. "If I find out, I'm sure I'll let you know." He again turned to leave.

"Wait," Decker said. "Detective Glass needs to escort you out. We'll be talking again soon. I suggest you don't leave town."

"I'm not going anywhere, detective. I have a father to bury."

Detective Glass was walking Joe from the bullpen and looked a little abashed when he said, "Mr. Nash, I know my partner can come on pretty strong sometimes."

"I can see that," Joe said. "Listen, my sister told me there would be an autopsy. I just wanted to know if it's been done. Why is this such a big deal with your partner?" It was apparent that Glass was playing his part in the old "good cop, bad cop" routine, but Joe figured he'd have a better chance of getting information from him than Decker.

"Alice O'Sullivan is our Deputy Coroner," Glass replied. "She handled the autopsy. I'll see what I can find out and let you know."

"When will we be able to see it?"

"That depends," Glass said. "If she declares your father's death to be of natural causes, then you can receive the report by making a simple written request as next of kin. But if she finds evidence of something else, she'll send a copy of the report to District Attorney Elaine Stewart. If Stewart declares the death a homicide, you might not be able to see the entire report for a while."

"A homicide?" Joe questioned. This was the first time anyone had come out and mentioned the word. "I thought it was a heart attack."

Glass seemed sincere when he answered, "I'm sure that's what it was. Like I said, I'll let you know what I find out."

Joe left, trying to imagine a gun in his dad's hand. The man was an asshole—but a gun? Something happened to his dad. Who had he become? Too many things didn't make sense.

CHAPTER 5

JOE HAD JUST returned to Alex's house when his cell rang.

"Hello."

"Is this Joe Nash?"

"Yes, who's calling?"

"My name is Anthony Gallo. I'm an attorney that was retained by your father. First off, I want to give my condolences to you and your sister on your loss. I understand this is a difficult time for both of you. Your father had given me instructions to contact you and your sister in the event of his death. He directed me to assist with the funeral arrangement, file probate requirements for his estate, and review some items he wished me to share with the two of you. When do you think you and your sister would be available to meet?"

"I would need to speak with her," Joe replied, "but I imagine this evening or sometime tomorrow."

"If agreeable with you, I'd like to do this as soon as possible. Could we meet at my office this evening at six?"

Gallo gave Joe his address on Daniel Island, and Joe agreed that he and Emily would be there that evening. He spent the next hour or so calling Dr. Wallace's office at Johns Hopkins, his manager, John Mercer, and his landlord letting them all know he'd be in Charleston the next few weeks. It was approaching noon when he left and made the ten-minute walk to meet Alex at the Old Town Grill.

He arrived early and was seated at a table next to one of the windows. He ordered an iced tea and started to relax a bit—the first time since it seemed like his career may have begun to unravel. Watching the diverse mix of people scurrying up and down King Street reminded Joe of how much he missed living in downtown Charleston. There was a vitality inherent in the city—a combination of the old and the new. Baseball and the city had always been one for Joe. His love for the game hadn't waned, but five years basically living out of a suitcase had taken its toll—not only on his psyche but also on his bank account. His $100,000 signing bonus was practically gone. Law school was always tugging at him, a little more since his elbow began to act up. He took the LSAT four years ago and scored in the top 10%. His score was only good for another year. Maybe it was time—time to accept the fact that his dream just wasn't going to happen.

Joe was staring in the middle distance when a voice said, "Hey, buddy. Sorry, I'm late. How'd your meeting go with that detective?"

Joe snapped out of it as Alex slid into the seat across from him. "Not so good. To be honest, I'm not all that impressed with the detectives I met this morning." Joe gave Alex a quick recount of his meeting—omitting any mention of the gun.

"I'm sure things will work out," Alex said. "Remember, I'm here if you need any help. Now, it's been a while since I've seen you. What's it like playing Triple-A ball?"

"These guys are terrific—especially the ones from Puerto Rico. I played down there the last two off-seasons. Alex, you wouldn't believe it. There are sixteen and seventeen-year-old kids who are just about Major League ready. The Orioles brought me up the last two spring trainings in Florida, and I got a chance to pitch to some big league studs like Francisco Lindor, Javier Báez, and Mookie Betts. And get this, I actually struck out Aaron Judge."

"That's cool, but here's the big question," Alex said. "Are you going to get that arm fixed? You've put in your time, buddy. You deserve it. God, Joe, one more move, and you're playing with the big boys!"

"We'll see. It's been a hell of a ride. I remember playing with guys in Class-A ball that could barely afford a decent meal. They'd play in front of ten thousand fans, and after the game, try to scrape up enough to eat. We'd all spend fifteen hours a day with our roommates and around twelve hours a day with everyone else. You root for your teammates, but you still hope you're better than them. It's bizarre, competing against your own teammates.

"It's crazy. Only about sixteen of the guys who started with the Tides this year are still on the team. I've played with almost 45 guys this season. Some were moved up, and some were sent back to Double-A. Some just got released, which is a bitch to see. But all that shit disappears the moment you step on the field."

Joe and Alex spent the next hour and a half talking baseball. They traded stories from their college days playing for the Cougars. It made no difference that they'd heard all the stories many times before. Finally, Alex checked his watch and said, "I need to run—got a two o'clock back at the office. I guess I'll see you tonight after you meet that lawyer."

~~~~

Joe was relaxing on the couch when he got a call from John Mercer. The Orioles had arranged for him to take X-rays and an MRI the following day at MUSC. The results would be sent to Dr. Wallace at Johns Hopkins.

Emily made it to the house that afternoon at about 3:30.

"How did it go this morning?" she asked.

Joe told her about his discussions and the surprise revelation of the gun.

"Decker's an ass. I'm not sure we'll get much from him, but Glass seems a bit more helpful. I know they told you that Dad had a heart attack, but I got the impression they think there's more to it than that. Detective Glass even used the word homicide. If they decide it was more than just a heart
~~~~

attack, they're going to be all over Dad's house. I figure we need to get out there today and see what we can find just in case that happens. Otherwise, we can forget about getting in there. Do you have a key to his house?"

"Sure."

"Great. I say we head out there now. Oh, and I almost forgot. I got a call from Dad's lawyer. His name is Anthony Gallo, and he's going to help with the funeral and other stuff that needs to be done. We've got an appointment with him to-night at six o'clock."

They left the house and drove across the Ravenel Bridge into Mt. Pleasant and followed Highway 17 about five miles to Snee Farm development. Joe turned onto Frank's street and suddenly stopped the truck. "Shit."

Four cruisers and a police van were parked out front. Three of the squad cars and the van were from Charleston. The remaining one carried the Mt. Pleasant Police insignia. "Damn it," Joe said. "They're already out here."

Joe pulled up and parked behind one of the squad cars. When they approached the front door, an officer stopped them. Needing to come up with something fast, Joe said, "Excuse me, officer. I'm Joe Nash, and this is my sister, Emily. This is our dad's house. We're just coming over to pick up some things our lawyer needs. What's going on?"

"You're going to have to wait here," the officer said and disappeared into the house. He returned a moment later, fol-lowed by Detective Glass.

"Detective, I'm glad you're here. I was explaining to your officer that we need to get into our Dad's house to get ..."

Glass interrupted Joe. "Come with me, please." He led Joe and Emily away from the front door to the sidewalk, where he stopped and said, "I'm afraid that's not going to happen. The house is now considered a crime scene."

"What do you mean a crime scene? I was telling your officer that our lawyer needs some documents in there."

"I was going to call you shortly," Glass said. "District Attorney Stewart has ruled your father's death a homicide."

"Wait a minute," Emily said. "Detective Decker told me my dad had a heart attack."

"I'm afraid the autopsy indicated otherwise," Glass quickly replied. "The deputy coroner found no evidence of cardio-vascular disease or cardiac arrest. Evidence indicated your father died of suffocation. Her report identified the presence of ruptured blood vessels in the eyes, highly elevated levels of carbon dioxide, and evidence of bruising around the nose and mouth."

"Wait a minute," Joe said. "So she's saying someone murdered our father?"

"All I'm saying is the Deputy Coroner O'Sullivan reported the cause of death to be suffocation, and District Attorney Stewart ruled the case to be a homicide."

"So, what happens now?" Joe asked.

"Well, this is a crime scene, and we're treating it that way. Our forensics team will analyze what evidence we currently have. When we finish searching the house and removing items pertinent to our investigation, it will be secured and taped. No one will be allowed inside the house until people from the coroner's office inventory its contents. Once that's done, the house will be resealed and remain closed for the balance of the investigation. Your father's office will be treated in the same way as his house."

"What about us?" Joe asked.

"You'll both need to come to the station and give formal statements. I'll need to check with my partner and let you know what time."

"All right, but what about our dad?" Joe asked. "I mean if the autopsy is finished, does that mean we can have his body released? We've got to make arrangements for the funeral."

"You should be okay," Glass answered. "I suggest you go ahead and contact the coroner in North Charleston."

There was nothing more that could be done, so Joe and Emily left and started back to Alex's. "I can't believe this is happening," Emily said. "What did he get into? Why would someone want to kill him?"

"Maybe that lawyer has some answers. I sure as hell don't." Joe checked his watch and saw it was approaching five. "Let's head over to Daniel Island."

CHAPTER 6

AFTER A LIGHT meal at The Dog and Duck, they drove to Anthony Gallo's office on the second floor of a small building located just down the road from their dad's office. They entered a good-sized reception room and approached an attractive young woman seated behind a sliding glass window. She slid open the window. "May I help you?"

"Hello. I'm Joe Nash. My sister and I have a meeting with Mr. Gallo."

"Certainly," she answered. "He's expecting you. Please have a seat, and I'll let him know you're here."

Lit by the soft glow of Tiffany lamps perched on leather inlaid end tables, the room emanated a subtle but rich warmth. Leather-backed chairs encircled the room with two oversized grayscale modern art paintings hung on opposing walls. Joe and Emily were seated for less than a minute before Mr. Gallo opened the door leading to the firm's inner offices.

"Good evening, folks. Thanks again for meeting at such short notice. I'm Anthony Gallo. Can I get you some coffee? Perhaps a soft drink or bottled water?" Both Joe and Emily declined, and Gallo continued, "All right then, if you'll come this way, please? We're set up down in the conference room."

He stood a shade over six-feet and was noticeably thin—almost to the point of looking sickly. His jet-black mane, offering a touch of gray, was combed straight back. A pale complexion evidenced an obsession with his work. He wore an impeccably tailored navy blue Armani suit—complimented by a gold tie and matching gold suspenders. He reminded Joe of one of those quintessential Hollywood movie lawyers.

They followed Gallo down a short hallway into a large room—much of it taken up by eight high-back leather chairs surrounding a mahogany conference table. Matching mahogany bookcases filled with thick red and gray hardback law journals lined the walls. Joe and Emily took seats on one side of the conference table. Gallo sat next to them at the head. He carefully opened a binder in front of him.

"Excuse me, Mr. Gallo," Joe said. "Before we start, we should probably have a copy of the agreement you and our dad signed."

"Certainly. And I commend you for asking." His eyes remained on Joe when he reached under the table, pressed a button, and said, "Ms. Hanson, please bring in the Nash agreement." He paused for a moment before continuing, "It's always been interesting to me that one of the major areas of fraud occurs around the time of the passing of a family member." The door opened, and the woman from the reception room entered and gave Gallo a folder.

"Thank you, Arlene." Gallo opened the folder. "Here we are." He removed a document and handed it to Joe.

Joe scanned the agreement, slid it in front of Emily, and pointed to the second sheet where Frank had signed and dated.

"That's his signature," Emily confirmed.

Gallo returned the agreement to the folder. "I'll have Ms. Hanson make a copy of this for you. Let's move on."

Before Gallo could continue, Joe said, "Excuse me, but I noticed my dad signed that less than a month ago."

"That's correct," Gallo said but made no further comment.

"It just seems strange he would make all those arrangements less than a month before he died. And I don't know if you're aware, but the police are calling this a homicide."

"Yes, I'm aware of that," Gallo answered—again choosing not to elaborate. After a somewhat awkward silence, Gallo began by explaining that Frank had arranged and paid for both his funeral and burial. "As executor of his estate, I've already contacted both the McAlister Funeral Home and Mt. Pleasant Memorial Gardens cemetery. The funeral will be held next Monday at ten. Your father specified that there was to be no church service, and only you two and a few of his close friends are to be at the cemetery." Gallo took a few moments describing the particulars of what will be done at the funeral home and the cemetery. He finished by saying that it would be necessary for either Joe or Emily to stop by the coroner's office and authorize the release of their father's body.

"I can do that," Joe said.

"Good," Gallo said. "I'll be filing a copy of your father's will and death certificate along with other documents with the probate court within the next week or so. I realize the process can be time-consuming and frustrating at times, so please don't hesitate to let me know should you have any questions."

"Excuse me," Emily said. "You just mentioned our dad's will. When will we see it?"

"Actually, that was the next item on the agenda," Gallo said and removed a copy of Frank Nash's Last Will and Testament.

Except for $10,000 that was to be given to his secretary, Michelle Rice, Frank's estate was to be divided equally between Joe and Emily. Frank had continued to live in the small three-bedroom house he'd purchased after his ex-secretary left him, and except for leasing a new BMW every two years, he appeared to live a relatively simple life. The house still carried a healthy mortgage, and when combined with his other assets, his estate only totaled about $100,000. Gallo explained that the probate process could take months to finalize. Also, specific assets involved in a homicide investigation are often frozen until released by the district attorney.

After Joe asked a few questions concerning the will, Gallo mentioned there was one final item he was required to address. He removed a simple No. 10 envelope from his binder and carefully placed it on the table as if it contained something fragile.

"Your father instructed me to give you this letter in the event of his death. I have no idea what it contains. He said it's 'for your eyes only' and should not be opened unless both of you are present and alone." He furtively slid the letter in front of Joe. For a moment, Joe seemed reluctant to touch it.

Gallo stood—giving both Joe and Emily his and his assistant's business cards. "That should be all for now. We'll keep you apprised as we work our way through the process. And please don't hesitate to contact either of us should you have any questions or concerns."

Emily had, for the most part, been quiet during the meeting. But as they were walking out, she stopped Gallo and said, "Excuse me, but I do have a question."

"Certainly, Ms. Nash."

"My brother told me you've worked for my dad for some time. I was just wondering if you noticed anything different about him lately."

Gallo half smiled and rather dismissingly said, "Perhaps, but I'm sure your father had a lot on his mind. You two have a nice evening. Ms. Hanson will show you out."

~~~~

As soon as Joe and Emily left, Gallo withdrew to his office and shut the door. He slid open a panel on the credenza behind his desk, exposing a biometric safe. Pressing his right thumb into
~~~~

the print pad, the door opened with a click. He removed a sealed manila envelope containing a short, hand-written note from Frank Nash and a disposable cell phone. The message read: ***Once you have given my children the letter, use this phone to call 345 555-3756 and say, "strike three, and you're out." Destroy the phone and note when you have completed the call.*** Having set up several international bank accounts for clients, Gallo recognized the Cayman Islands area code.

The call was answered on the second ring. Gallo passed on the message, and after a curt "thank you," the line went dead. He then destroyed both the hand-written note and the cell phone.

Twelve hundred miles due south, a banker in Belize City, Belize sat in front of his computer and, using instructions from Frank Nash, first moved the Cayman Islands funds to the SPARKASSE BANK in Malta. He then deposited the funds into a shell company he had previously created. For the next hour, the money traveled from Malta to a series of private banks in Panama, Switzerland, and Barbados—each transfer carrying a new account number and passcode. The final destination for the money was the SCOTIABANK in Belize City, Belize.

~~~~

By the time Joe and Emily left Gallo's office, dark clouds had begun gathering over the Atlantic, and the wind had picked up.
~~~~

Back in the Ranger, Emily turned to Joe. "So, what do we do now?"

Joe held the letter up. "One way to find out. Should we open it?"

Emily was the inquisitive one—always wondering what's around the next bend in the road. "Heck yes," she said, her curiosity in overdrive. "Go ahead!"

Joe carefully opened the envelope and removed a single sheet. He unfolded it and began to read.

***

Dear Joe & Emily,

If you are reading this, you have met Anthony Gallo, and I am no longer living. You can trust Mr. Gallo, but you mustn't share the contents of this letter with him or anyone else.

My life is in danger. You must make no attempt to find out why. All you need to know is there are certain things in my life I've had to keep secret.

I realize I have been a failure as a father to both of you. I am truly ashamed of that. I was foolish to treat your mother the way I did. She was a wonderful woman, and while I did not often show it, I loved her. I have been selfish and regret the pain I have caused all of you. I live with that every day.

Joe ... I have always been proud of you. I now realize I tried to be more of a coach than a father—

*and failed at both. I apologize for whatever damage
my actions have caused.*

*Emily ... you have grown into a remarkably
intelligent and lovely woman. I sincerely apologize
for not being there when you needed me most.*

*If I could turn back the clock, I would. I don't
expect that you will forgive the way I've treated you
or your mother. I never said it enough, but I love you
both and wish you nothing but the best for the rest of
your lives.*

Love,
Dad

*P.S ... Joe, check your favorite player's card. That
card just went way up in value.*
P.S.S ... You <u>must</u> destroy this letter after reading it.

***

Joe and Emily were quiet for a time—both trying to come
to grips with the letter.

"So, what do you think?" Emily asked. "Dad just
apologized."

"It's a little late if you ask me. And what the hell is that
about keeping part of his life secret? What secret is he talking
about?"

"I have no idea," Emily said, "but it clearly had something to do with his death. And what was that about a baseball card?"

"He was obviously talking about Randy Johnson. He knew he's my favorite player. Hell, I don't even know where my card collection is anymore."

"All the cards are at Dad's house," Emily said. "He used one of the second-floor bedrooms as an office and kept them in the closet along with your old gloves and bats and trophies."

"Well, it's pretty obvious he's trying to tell me something," Joe offered.

"I wonder why he didn't just put the card with that letter," Emily asked. "And what do you think he meant about the card going way up in value?"

"I'm not sure," Joe said. "Maybe because I would be the only one who knows about Randy Johnson being my favorite player. And the 'up in value' thing sounds like it has something to do with money." After a short pause, Joe slapped the steering wheel and bemoaned, "Aw, shit! There's no way we're getting in there. That house is sealed up."

Emily smiled and said, "Oh, I don't know about that."

"What do you mean?"

"The latch on my old bedroom window broke years ago. You can open it from the outside."

"Yeah," Joe said, "but you've been gone more than two years. How do you know Dad hasn't fixed it?"

Emily laughed. "Dad fix something? Come on—he doesn't even know which end of a hammer to use. I used to sneak in and out of that window all through high school. I'll bet money that latch is still broken. There's an oak tree in the back-yard. One of its limbs is right next to the roof. I used to climb out on it and hop onto the roof. Piece of cake."

"What happens if we get caught?" Joe asked.

"I never got caught in high school. Plus, it's our house, and it's not like we're going to steal anything that's not already ours."

Joe couldn't get over how brash Emily sounded. He smiled and said, "What happened to my shy little sister?"

"She grew up!" Emily shot back.

His smile disappeared. "Emily, you're not in high school anymore, and don't forget; the house is a crime scene!"

"Come on, Joe. We need to do this."

Joe thought for a moment. "I guess you're right. And Dad wouldn't have said anything about that card if he didn't want us to get it. Yeah, I'm in. We can do this later tonight, but let's just make sure we don't get caught. I'd rather not go to jail."

CHAPTER 7

IT WAS A little before 8:00 Wednesday evening when Joe dropped Emily off at her apartment and returned to Alex's. When he shut the door, he saw a note taped to the back of it: "Meet me at Mellow Mushroom." Joe had to laugh. Alex and his college roommates would plaster the back of their front door with notes to each other.

It had been a long day, and Joe was in no mood for a bar. He'd hoped to catch a few hours of sleep before picking up Emily and heading out to try the old latch on her bedroom window. But on second thought, a beer with Alex might offer a needed break from the chaos experienced the last few days. He left and made the five-minute walk.

The Mushroom was already filling up, and after a quick survey of the place, Joe spotted Alex at the far end of the bar talking to a girl. He gauged her to be in her mid-twenties, tall, fit, long blond hair—the type of woman who demands a second look.

Alex waved Joe over and said, "Joe, meet Shannon King. Shannon, meet my good friend, Joe Nash."

Shannon glanced up at Joe, who was immediately taken in by her flawless complexion and piercing blue eyes—eyes so blue they put a clear summer's sky to shame.

She smiled. "Hi, Joe. Alex has been talking my ear off about you. I feel like we're old friends."

Joe grinned. "Well, Alex has never been at a loss for words, that's for sure. It's a pleasure to meet you, Shannon."

Alex caught sight of a bartender and ordered three drafts.

Shannon's smile faded, and her face turned serious. She put her hand on Joe's forearm and said, "Alex told me about your father. I'm so sorry."

"Thanks. I appreciate that." They were both under the impression that Frank had a heart attack. This wasn't the time or the place to talk about a murder investigation. Hell, he wasn't sure what was going on anyway. His dad had a secret life that probably got him killed. He happened to glance past Alex, and his eyes fell on a framed poster on the wall. Joe had to smile. The poster read:

**What sane person
could live in this world
and not be crazy?**

The bartender brought the beers. Alex picked his up and said, "Here's hoping Joe gets that arm patched up and makes it to the Show." The three clinked their mugs together. "So, how'd everything go today?"

"It went okay." It was the last thing Joe felt like talking about. He turned to Shannon and quickly changed the subject. "I don't know if Alex told you what a great catcher he was in college. Knowing him, I imagined he has."

Shannon laughed. "Oh, yes. He's constantly reminding me." She gave Alex a sly smile. "We all know how modest he is."

For the next hour, Joe was able to set aside the turmoil as Alex and he traded more stories from their playing days—Shannon enjoying every minute of it.

After a while, Joe checked his watch, swigged the last of his beer, and announced, "Guys, this has been fun, but I'm going to call it a night. I've got a bunch of stuff to do tomorrow."

"All right, buddy. I'll see you back at the house."

Joe was a little surprised when Shannon gave him a hug and a peck on the cheek. "I'm so glad I finally got to meet you. If you need a break to take your mind off things, some of us are meeting up at Magnolia's Friday night. I know you're going to be busy, but it would be great if you could join us."

"We'll see how things go, but it sounds like fun," Joe said. "It was great to meet you, Shannon."

<p style="text-align:center">~~~~</p>

Joe was up at 2:30 a.m. in the kitchen quietly making a cup of coffee when he heard, "Jesus, Joe. It's the middle of the night, and you're making coffee?"

"Sorry if I woke you, buddy."

"No problem. Is everything all right?"

Joe had known Alex for almost ten years and trusted him implicitly. He felt an urge to tell him something but couldn't talk about his father's letter or the late-night escapade he and Emily had planned.

"Listen," he started, "I need to do something tonight, and I can't tell you what it is. Some things have come up since my dad died, and I need to deal with them myself. You're just going to have to trust me on this one."

Alex's confusion was tempered with concern. "Okay, okay. I get it. But whatever it is, you know I'm here to help."

"I know. I've got to go now but should be back in an hour or two. Thanks for understanding."

The wind had picked up, and a light but steady rain was falling when Joe pulled up in front of Emily's duplex. He looked twice before he spotted her, dressed in all black from head to toe—complete with a black backpack and stocking hat! She jumped in the front seat, and Joe shook his head.

"Em, you look like a cat burglar."

"Well, you said you didn't want to get caught, right?"

"Right. That's the plan. Hey, do you have class tomorrow?"

"Yeah, until around one o'clock. But, like I said, I can skip it if you need me to."

"No, you go on to class. I'll stop by the coroner's office in the morning and sign whatever I need to. I'm supposed to be at MUSC at noon for some x-rays and an MRI on my arm. That shouldn't take more than an hour. Remember, the detective said we need to give our statements. I figure we can meet at Alex's after your class and make it over to the Lockwood station around two o'clock. If it's okay with you, I'll call Glass and tell him we'll be there then."

"That works," Emily said.

At this time on a weeknight, there were only a few cars on the road as they crossed the Ravenel Bridge into Mt. Pleasant. The Snee Farm streets were deserted, and the sidewalks glistened under the streetlights, the windshield wipers slapped back and forth, and the fronds on the palms that lined the lawns crackled in the wind. Joe parked three or four houses down from his dad's house.

"Okay," he said, "make sure you bring your cell and turn the ringer down. I'll stay around the house and call you if there's a problem. You remember what the box looks like, right?"

"Sure," Emily said.

"Good. All the cards are in alphabetical order."

"Relax," Emily said, "I'll just put the whole thing in my backpack. That'll be quicker."

Their dad's house, like the rest on the street, was completely dark. As they made their way up the driveway to the rear of the house, they saw yellow police tape crisscrossing the front door.

In the backyard, Joe stopped at the base of the oak tree. "Okay, Em. It's wet, so be careful up there."

"I'll be fine," she said and began scaling. Her agility impressed Joe as she nimbly made her way up and out onto the thick limb that hung next to the rear eave. She dropped onto the roof and proceeded to crawl up toward her bedroom dormer. The rain had intensified, and Joe could barely see Emily until she got to the window. She turned, gave him the thumbs-up, and disappeared into the house.

Emily turned on her cell phone light and made her way down the hallway. She walked past the stairs and stopped. She got the chills realizing it had been less than forty-eight hours since her dad's body was discovered down there. She shook it off and entered his office. Just as she remembered, there were two boxes of cards on the shelf in the closet. Each was 2 ½" x 3 ½" x 20" and held over 500 trading cards. Emily removed her backpack and slid the boxes inside. Before zipping it up, she noticed a small cardboard box in the closet holding a few baseballs. She found one signed by all the players from Joe's senior year in college and tossed it inside the pack before closing it up.

It had only been a few minutes since Emily disappeared inside, but Joe was already getting nervous. He was still under the tree when he noticed headlights creeping down the street. The car passed, and Joe held his breath. Sliding behind a row of bushes, Joe watched a police cruiser come to a stop next to his truck. It stayed a moment before moving past the truck, turning around, and stopping directly behind the Ranger. It remained there for a minute before the door opened, and an officer emerged with a flashlight. He shined the light into the truck's rear cabin and then into the front. He continued past the driver's side door and slid something under the wiper.

Joe remained frozen behind the bushes as he watched the officer return to his car and drive on down the windswept street, eventually disappearing into the night.

Joe tried to settle his nerves. It was eerily quiet—except for the rain and the pounding of his heart. Suddenly, something touched the back of his neck. He almost jumped out of his shoes and whirled around—only to see his sister's smiling face. "Mission accomplished!" she proudly proclaimed.

Joe grabbed his chest. "Holy shit, Em. You scared the be-jesus out of me!"

"Sorry about that. I got the stuff. Let's get out of here."

They jogged back to the truck, and Joe removed the small plastic bag holding a parking ticket from the window before getting in. They were both completely soaked. He started the engine and pulled away from the curb when Emily saw the ticket and started to laugh. "Well, big brother, I guess we got busted after all."

"Yeah, and if they check that parking ticket, they'll know I was here."

"I wouldn't worry about that," Emily said. "Nobody knows we were here, so nobody's going to check a parking ticket. Just pay it, and we'll be fine."

"I guess that makes sense," Joe said. "You got the cards, right?"

"Yep." Emily slipped off her pack and pulled out the autographed ball. "I thought this might bring back some memories."

Joe recognized it immediately. "God, Em, I completely forgot about this. Thanks. I'll pull off somewhere, and we can check out Randy Johnson's card."

Joe exited Snee Farm and turned into the deserted Town Centre Shopping Mall. He parked in front of Grimaldi's Pizzeria. Emily removed the two boxes and handed them to Joe. The cards were arranged in alphabetical order, and he quickly identified the Randy Johnson card. When he removed it, he found a small piece of white paper taped to it—another note from their dad. It was a series of letters and numbers above the words: *first year, final year, number.*

NOSCBZBSXXX3736626374

Usher

first year ... final year ... number

Joe stared at the paper—clueless about what it meant except that the words at the bottom probably referred to Randy Johnson. He checked the back of the card. Johnson's rookie year in the majors was 1988, his final year was 2007, and his number was 51. "Em, look at this. That's 1988-2007-51. Might be some sort of combination or code."

He studied the 21 letters and numbers at the top of the paper but couldn't make head nor tails out of what they meant. "This is all pretty hard to believe. Codes from the grave from our murdered dad."

"What does Usher mean?" Emily asked.

Joe shook his head. "I'm not sure."

Joe handed the paper to Emily. "All right, there should be a pen and some paper in the glove compartment. Make yourself a copy of this." Emily wrote down the information on the back of a Jiffy Lube receipt. Joe waited until she was finished. "It's obvious Dad thought we could figure all this out. But whatever it means, we're not going to do it in the middle of an empty parking lot at four o'clock in the morning. We're soaked, cold, and tired. I say we head on back and deal with this later today."

CHAPTER 8

JOE'S CELL JOLTED him awake at eight the next morning. He'd been asleep for a shade over three hours and mumbled, "Hello."

"Nash, this is Detective Decker. I need you and your sister down at the station in an hour. Need your formal statements. Nine o'clock—both of you."

"Your partner told us about the statements, but I've got to be at the coroner's this morning. Plus, my sister is in class. I figure we should be able to get there around two."

The phone was quiet except for Decker's exaggerated breathing until he finally grumbled, "Two o'clock then." The line went dead.

Now that Joe was awake, he rolled out of bed, shuffled to the kitchen, and made some coffee. Sitting at the kitchen table, he couldn't get over the fact that his dad's "secret" life had probably cost him his life. And then there was the gun in the kitchen. And the letter. And the baseball card and the code attached to it. *What the hell does this all mean—what do those letters, numbers, and words mean? And that code: 1988-2009-51. What was Dad trying to tell me?*

His frustration growing, he left the thought unfinished and got ready for his meeting with the coroner.

~~~~

After a short wait, Joe met Deputy Coroner Alice O'Sullivan, and she led him back to her office. O'Sullivan was a short, portly woman with a thicket of unkempt, steel-gray hair. Despite her obvious medical credentials and prominent position, she reminded Joe of Aunt Bee from the old Andy Griffith Show. After exchanging some pleasantries, Joe signed the consent form releasing his father's body so it could be transported to the funeral home.

"Detective Glass told me my dad was suffocated," Joe said. "Did you learn anything else from the autopsy that might help find out who did this?"

O'Sullivan's body language gave Joe the distinct impression that she didn't want to answer.

"As next of kin, you're certainly entitled to the full autopsy report, but that won't be ready for a while. For now, we can provide a Provisional Anatomical Diagnosis. It contains the cause of death and some general details I observed while performing the autopsy, but it won't have all the histology and
~~~~

toxicology results. I've sent that preliminary report to the detectives working your case."

She explained that police sometimes withhold evidence from the public to help determine whether suspects are guilty. If a suspect possesses nonpublic information, police reason, it's likely he or she either committed the crime or at least knows who might have.

"So, there's something you're not telling me?"

"No, not necessarily—only that you'll need to talk to the detectives. The full autopsy report is normally available to the family in a month or two. However, this is a homicide, and you should get it quicker than that."

"How much quicker?"

"That depends on the detectives."

Joe left O'Sullivan's office feeling even more confused and distrustful of the police. He was also feeling a wave of mounting anger toward his father. It was clear he was murdered because of a secret kept from his family—a secret he didn't want Emily and him to discover. But why would he give him a clue about the Randy Johnson trading card and the piece of paper attached to it?

Joe's MRI and X-ray appointment at the hospital took less than an hour. He was told he could expect a call from Johns Hopkins Hospital with the results of the tests. He was again feeling overwhelmed—everything seemed to be happening at once. Too many unanswered questions, too many secrets.

He got back to the house around one and was surprised to find Emily making a sandwich in the kitchen. "Em, how did you get in here?"

"Alex gave me a key. He figured I'd be spending time here with you, and it would be easier for all of us."

"That makes sense. How about making a sandwich for me?"

"Absolutely."

He filled her in about the nonevent at the coroner's office while she whipped up another sandwich.

"It looks like we'll have to rely on Detectives Decker and Glass to tell us what happened," Joe said.

"Well, I guess we'll know soon," Emily said. "Eat your sandwich, and let's head over to the police station."

~~~~

While waiting to give their statements at Lockwood, Joe leaned toward Emily and whispered, "I figure they'll put us in separate rooms. We know the detectives have the preliminary autopsy report, so we need to press them for details."

They settled in and waited … and waited. After half an hour, Joe asked the desk sergeant how much longer it would be.

The sergeant's weather-beaten eyes and face reflected too many years on the force. "Well, now, I would imagine someone will come out to get you when they come out to get you."
~~~~

Joe stared up at the sergeant. "That was helpful," he said and returned to his seat.

"What did he say?" Emily asked.

"He doesn't know."

The wait lasted another twenty minutes before Detective Glass appeared and ushered them into the bullpen. He walked them past the individual cubicles to the far end of the room, where there were two small conference rooms.

"Mr. Nash, you can go in there, and Detective Decker will be with you shortly." He gestured for Emily to follow him into the second room.

Joe took a seat. The room was stark—just a metal table and four metal chairs, a single overhead light, and a large mirror on the right wall. It was cold, too. Joe knew the steel chairs, two-way mirror, and temperature were all designed to make a suspect uncomfortable—but he wasn't a suspect. Still, he couldn't understand why Decker had been so antagonistic.

About five minutes later, Decker came into the room with a curt, "I have some questions for you."

"I told you I'd do whatever I can to help," Joe began, "but I'm not sure how much I can offer. I've told you several times that I haven't seen or talked to my father in five years."

"All right then, let's talk about why you haven't had any contact with him. It's fairly normal for sons to have disagreements with their fathers when they're growing up. But why did you hate him so much?"

"I never said I hated my dad. I only said I had nothing to do with him."

Decker put his head to one side and spread his hands apart. "And just why would a son have nothing to do with his father, Mr. Nash?"

Joe wasn't sure whether Decker was sarcastic or merely inquisitive—either way, he didn't like where this was going. "I thought he mistreated my mother and turned his back on my sister and me. That's all."

"Interesting," Decker said and leaned closer to Joe. "Sounds like you were pretty pissed off at your old man. Did you ever think about making him pay for all those things he did to you and your family?"

"Listen to me, detective. I told you I'd do what I can to help find out who did this to my dad. But I'm not going to sit here and listen to you accuse me of having anything to do with his death. That's ridiculous, and you know it. This isn't accomplishing anything."

Decker sat back and feigned surprise. "Mr. Nash, don't be so defensive. I'm only trying to understand your relationship with your father." Before Joe could respond, Decker pressed forward. "I was also wondering about your dad's will. You know, like insurance policies, stocks—things like that. I imagine you and your sister stand to inherit a good bit of that. Am I right, Mr. Nash?"

"Jesus Christ, Decker. I think we're finished here."

Joe got up to leave. "Mr. Nash, please sit down." Decker's voice was now much more conciliatory. "You have to understand that as far as I'm concerned, everyone is a suspect—until they're not. You know I've got to ask those questions. Just relax, and let's finish this up. I only have a few more questions."

Joe was still pissed but reluctantly sat down.

"We know your dad divorced your mother before she died of cancer. Did he leave her for another woman?"

"Yes," Joe answered. "He was having an affair with his secretary, but it only lasted a short time. I would have no idea if he were ever involved with anyone else."

Decker had a few more peripheral questions about his dad's business and the .38 found in his kitchen. Then he finally said, "That's all I have for today. I'm sure we'll talk again. I'll take you out to the lobby."

Decker started to stand, but Joe remained seated and said, "Our father was murdered, and we don't know anything. I think my sister and I deserve to know what happened to our dad."

"You'll be able to see the preliminary autopsy report within a few days," Decker answered.

"Come on," Joe quickly said. "Treat us like humans. What aren't you telling us?"

Decker was quiet, debating how much to offer. "Okay, we're still working on the investigation, but there is one thing."

"And what's that?" Joe asked.

"The coroner found traces of polyethylene inside your father's mouth. A plastic bag was used to suffocate him, and our forensic techs know the specific type and source of the bag used. I'm telling you this, but you and your sister mustn't share it with anyone."

"I understand," Joe said. "Anything else?"

"At this point, no. But we should get the complete autopsy shortly. We'll see what that shows."

"All right," Joe said, "but please let us know what else you learn."

Decker nodded and stood. "Come with me. I need to walk you out."

Emily wasn't in the lobby, and Joe took a seat waiting for her to finish her meeting with Glass. He didn't wait long before they appeared. The detective thanked both of them for coming in before retreating to the bullpen.

They were barely out of the door when Emily asked, "How did it go?"

"Well, the son-of-a-bitch started off by insinuating we might have been involved in Dad's death. Things eventually settled down, and I asked if he learned anything new from the autopsy."

"The plastic bag, right?"

"Exactly. Traces of polyurethane. Did Glass tell you anything else?"

"He said whoever killed Dad knew what they were doing. He called it a 'professional hit.' Glass said whoever did it wore gloves and 'wiped down' the house. The only fingerprints on the gun were Dad's. His computer and cell were missing, and all of his security cameras were removed. Glass said the coroner established the time of death to be somewhere between 24 and 48 hours before his secretary found him Tuesday morning."

"God, Em," Joe said. "That means he was probably killed sometime Sunday or Monday morning."

"That's what they think."

The thought of his dad lying dead in his living room while he was pitching Monday night gave him a sickening feeling.

"Wasn't any security camera footage saved anywhere?" Joe asked.

"No. Dad had one of those systems that only downloaded to your cell phone and computer. He never trusted the Cloud."

"All this stuff is interesting," Joe said, "but it sounds like they have no idea who did it. I've heard if the cops don't arrest someone or at least find a critical clue in the first forty-eight hours, the chances of solving murders are cut in half."

They had just made it to the truck when Emily started to cry. Joe put his arm around her and whispered, "It's going to be okay, Sis."

"No, it's not," she said, her voice cracking. "Damn it, Joe. Every time I hear someone say 'murder' or 'killer,' I can't believe they're talking about Dad. He may not have been the greatest father, but he was the only one we had."

"I know, Em. I know. But maybe the clue we found on the back of that card will help us figure out what happened to Dad."

"Maybe we should tell the detectives about the card," Emily offered.

"Maybe," Joe replied, "but Dad was obviously trying to tell us something. I'm not saying we won't tell the police; all I'm saying is we need some more time to figure it out. And I get the feeling there's money involved. I think the note attached to that card has clues. It might be a combination to a safe or something like that."

"That's possible," Emily said, "but whatever it was, it got him killed."

"I promise we'll be careful," Joe said. "I say give it another day, and if we can't figure it out by then, we'll take it to the cops. Come on, let's go back. I say we work on that note for a while, and then I'll take you out for something to eat. Dinner is on me. What do you say?"

Emily gave her brother a weak smile. "Okay, plus dinner sounds good." Her smile broadened. "Plus, I'm broke, so you'll have to pay for it anyway."

Alex hadn't returned from work when they made it back to his house. After wrestling for an hour with what the note meant, they walked down to the Kickin' Chicken on King Street. When they sat down, Joe said, "No talk about detectives, investigations, baseball cards, or anything else like that. Agreed?"

"Agreed," Emily quickly answered. They had a pleasant meal—without a word spoken about what happened to their father or the investigation.

Joe walked Emily back to her apartment, and when he returned to the house, Alex was there. After having a beer with him, he went straight to bed for some well-deserved sleep.

~~~~
~~~~

Five years ago, Frank Nash began working for Eli Coldwell. It started by Nash only doing Coldwell's taxes and managing some of his investments. Soon, his involvement expanded when Coldwell and two of his associates had him funnel money into an offshore account in the Cayman Islands. It didn't take long for Frank to discover the money was coming from the drug, loan sharking, and prostitution businesses that Coldwell and his friends were operating in Charleston.

A little over a month ago, Coldwell discovered that Nash was secretly planning on leaving the operation and possibly taking what he knew to the authorities. There was no question that Frank Nash needed to be eliminated. But the problem Coldwell and his associate faced was that Nash had handled the organization and transfers of all the funds, and Coldwell did not wholly understand the intricacies of the process. It took some time for him to become comfortable with the consolidation and transfer the funds to the offshore account.

A few days ago, Coldwell met with his associates, and it was agreed that Frank Nash needed to be permanently removed before he took what he knew to the government. Arrangements were made, and the hit was carried out by one of Coldwell's most trusted men.

It was well past midnight. Eli Coldwell sat at the computer in the office of his small but well-appointed Broad Street house in downtown Charleston. A single lamp illuminated his desk—the rest of the room shrouded in darkness.

Coldwell entered the account number and password for his Cayman Islands account and stared at the screen—confusion spreading across his face.

"What the fuck?"

It showed a zero balance. Coldwell referred to his notes and reentered the account number and password but found the same result—nothing. His third attempt offered no solace—the account was completely wiped out. No money.

"Impossible," he seethed.

He sat there for a time, checking and rechecking the account, unable to understand what happened. Other than himself and his Cayman banker, the only person with access to that account was Frank Nash, and he was dead.

His two other associates had trusted him with their money—dirty money from drugs, loan sharking, and prostitution. And his associates were not known for their forgiving nature.

Who else could have had access to those codes? The only other person close to Frank Nash was his secretary, Michelle Rice.

He picked up his phone.

CHAPTER 9

JOE AND HIS sister had agreed the night before to meet at eleven o'clock for a quick lunch before her afternoon class.

He had some time to kill and took a walk around the College of Charleston campus. The walk brought back a myriad of memories from his four years at the school. There were the all-nighters studying for exams or finishing essays he'd put off for weeks. And then there were the parties—not to mention those Southern girls with their Southern ways. Although baseball was his focus, he was thankful for the education and the professors who helped him discover his intellectual potential. But more than anything, it was the friendships he treasured most—friendships he knew he would carry with him long after his college days were over.

He met Emily outside of the Math & Science Building at eleven, and the two of them walked to City Bistro. They had just sat down when Emily's cell rang.

She rustled through her backpack and pulled it out. "Hello." She looked a bit surprised and confused. "Yes, of course, I remember."

"Who is it?" Joe mouthed.

Emily held up her hand and shook her head. She continued listening carefully for the next few moments. Then she said, "Why?" A pause and then, "I'm sure I can. What time?" Another pause. "Okay, I'll be there." She disconnected the call.

"Who was it?"

The confusion was evident in her voice when she answered, "Michelle Rice."

"Dad's secretary, right?"

"Right. She wants to meet me tonight. Decker had her down at the police station yesterday afternoon. We must have just missed her. But get this. She said she has something about Dad she wants to tell me but wouldn't say it over the phone. She sounded nervous—almost terrified."

"Terrified? It obviously has something to do with Dad's murder. Maybe she thinks she's a target now. Where does she want to meet?"

"At Taco Boy down on Huger Street at seven o'clock. She said she'd feel safer when there's a lot of people around. I'll meet her at the bar."

"More weirdness," Joe said. "I guess we'll find out what's up tonight. Listen, I'm going to stop by the funeral home and cemetery to make sure everything's set for Monday. I'll pick you up at 6:45, and we'll go see what she has to say."

They finished their meals, speculating about what Michelle Rice might tell them.

~~~~

It was only a five-minute drive to the restaurant. When they arrived, most of the family crowd had departed, their territory claimed by an eclectic mix of college kids, after-work business suits, and a smattering of tattooed bikers.

Emily grabbed Joe's hand and edged through the crowd into the bar area.

"Do you see her?" Joe asked.

"Hang on. I'm looking." She surveyed the packed bar, then spotted Rice at the far end. "There she is."

Emily waved at Rice, but Rice shook her head and made no other effort to acknowledge her. Somewhat confused, Emily continued moving through the crowd toward the bar.

Rice was tall and on the thin side. Her light brown hair was tied back, and she wore a loose-fitting black dress. Joe gauged her to be in her mid-fifties and thought her attractive— in an understated, conservative way.

Emily approached with an awkward, "We made it. Do you want to get a table?"

"No," Rice answered—her eyes canvassing the crowd.

It was difficult to hear over the cacophony of music and crowd noise, and Emily had to raise her voice when introducing her brother.
~~~~

Rice nodded at Joe.

Without looking directly at Emily, Rice said, "I didn't know you would bring your brother. Wait a minute and then meet me in the restroom."

Joe watched her leave and asked, "What's going on?"

"I'm not sure. Wait here, and I'll find out what's up." Emily turned and followed Rice—leaving Joe alone and befuddled.

Emily entered the bathroom and found Rice standing against the far wall. "I'm sorry about all this," Rice said. "It's easier to talk in here."

"That's all right."

"Well, first of all, let me say that I know you and your brother had problems with your father, but you need to know he loved you."

Emily nodded. "The detective told me they thought he'd died a day or two before you found him. You told me you had something important to tell me. What is it?"

"All right," Rice began, "Something happened to your father over the last month or two. I don't know what it was, but I'd never seen him like that."

"What do you mean?"

"Well, it started with little things, like spending more time in his office with the door shut. He always took pride in how he looked, but it was clear he wasn't taking care of himself. I know he wasn't getting enough sleep, and he seemed nervous. He was definitely losing weight. He got more and more paranoid and even changed the locks on the office doors last week."

"Didn't you ask him what was going on?"

"Of course, I did. We were always very open about things, but he'd brush me off. Anyway, during the last month, he started to get these calls from people who wouldn't give me their names. A few weeks before your father died, he took two trips to Belize. Your dad hated flying and would always drive to the seminars and trade meetings he attended. I booked the flights, but he wouldn't tell me why he was going or who he was meeting. The whole thing was confusing. I would get upset with him, but it didn't do any good. It was like a wall came up between us."

"Did you tell Detective Decker all this?"

"I did," Rice answered. "Well, everything except the trips to Belize. Frank said, whatever I do, I was not to tell anyone about those trips. He made me promise. I thought it might have had something to do with Mr. Coldwell, but your dad said no."

"Who's Coldwell?"

"Frank met him at a College of Charleston baseball luncheon years ago. Coldwell started giving Frank money to invest. He's our biggest client now. Well, he's practically our only client. Frank used to handle taxes and investments for several people and small businesses. Then we started to get some of Coldwell's business. Then we got more and more of it, and pretty soon, some of the smaller accounts began to slip away.

"Your dad didn't like Coldwell—their relationship was strictly business. He did a lot of international investing for Mr. Coldwell, but I never got involved with that."

"What exactly does Coldwell do?"

"He and his associates own some restaurants and bars, but the bulk of their money came from criminal activities—drugs and things like that."

"God, you're telling me Dad was involved in drugs?"

"It didn't start out like that," Rice said. "At first, all of Coldwell's money came from his restaurant. After a while, he told Frank his associates had some additional funds to move offshore. By the time Frank figured out where the money was coming from, he told Coldwell he wanted out, but it was too late. Coldwell said if he left or went to the authorities, his associates would be 'upset.' It was clear to us that 'upset' meant they would hurt both of us and our families. We had no choice."

"Did you tell the detective about Coldwell?"

"No, I was so nervous," Rice answered. "I didn't know what to say and what not to say. I'm really scared. Ever since Frank was killed—I have the feeling someone's been following me. Maybe it's my imagination, but I can't shake it."

"If that's the case," Emily said, "you need to definitely tell the police as soon as possible."

"You're right," Rice replied. "I'll call Detective Decker. I'm sorry about all this. I just didn't know what to do."

"It's been difficult for all of us."

Emily was still trying to come to grips with the fact that her father was involved in criminal activities. Rice brought her back when she said, "I'm going to go now. Wait a minute before you leave."

Emily did as she was told before joining her brother at the bar.

"Well?" Joe said.

"That was strange," Emily replied and passed on the things Rice told her about their father.

"Jesus," Joe said, "I can't believe it. With everything he did to Mom and the family, I never would have thought he'd ever get involved with drugs. That has to be why he was killed."

"Yeah, and she said Dad went to Belize twice. Why in the world would he go there?"

"I have no idea," Joe said. "I don't even know where the hell Belize is. But I bet it also had something to do with what happened to him. Come on, let's get out of here."

Joe was dropping off Emily when she said, "I've got my first mid-term early next Tuesday morning, and I promised my study group I'd meet with them this evening. You're on your own tonight. Just call me if anything comes up."

"For sure," Joe said, "and don't leave your place without calling me first. I promised Alex I'd stop by Magnolia's tonight. I'm not excited about it. I'm just going to make an appearance and should be back by 9:30 if you need me."

CHAPTER 10

MAGNOLIA'S IS LOCATED in the original Charleston Customs House site built in 1739—its dining room dominated by its high ceilings and dark wood finishes. It was also known to be one of Charleston's priciest eateries.

Wearing a sports shirt and a pair of khaki slacks, Joe felt a little underdressed when he arrived at the restaurant. Alex, Shannon, and three other couples were already seated, and he took the only empty chair, which was between Shannon and an older gentleman in a navy-blue blazer.

Alex introduced the man in the blazer and his wife. "Joe, meet James and Mary Newberry. James is a partner at Donaldson, Chaney, and Ellis." He went on to make the other introductions. The waiter had just finished passing out cocktails and asked Joe if he'd like something to drink. He ordered a glass of Pinot Noir.

Alex turned to Joe and said, "I was just telling them we played ball together at the college and how you're on your way to the big leagues."

Joe smiled at the group, knowing he would now be the center of the conversation. "I'm not sure about that, but I certainly wouldn't complain if it happened."

"I remember when you played for the Cougars," Newberry said. "I actually watched you pitch a few times over at Patriots Point stadium. Impressive. Who drafted you?"

"The Baltimore Orioles. I'm with their Triple-A affiliate in Newport."

"Good for you, Joe," Newberry said. "I hope you make that next move to the majors."

Joe listened as the two other men at the table told stories of when they played high school ball. Joe simply nodded and smiled—everyone has their glory days.

Newberry caught Joe off guard when he said, "Alex mentioned to me that you've shown some interest in pursuing a law degree after your baseball days are over."

"I've thought about it, sir. But I'm focused on playing ball now, and hopefully, I won't have to make that decision for some time to come."

"I'm sure you're right," Newberry said, "but keep me in mind when that time comes."

After fending off a couple uncomfortable comments on the use of steroids in baseball, Joe answered a few more questions about his career until the conversation moved on to other subjects. He passed on the second round of drinks, and a short time later, the waiter arrived at the table to take the dinner orders.

Aware that Alex had told the group that his dad had recently passed, Joe stood and said, "I apologize, but I'm going to have to leave you folks. It's been fairly exhausting the last few days, but I'm glad I had the chance to meet all of you."

Alex stood. "I'll walk you out, Joe." When they reached the maître d' station, Alex stopped. "Thanks for coming, Joe. I know you've been busy, but I'm glad you had a chance to meet Newberry. He's a heavy hitter. I've got no doubt you can still make it with Baltimore, but I know you've got law school in the back of your mind. If and when that happens, make sure you let Newberry know. He got his law degree from the University of South Carolina, and he can pull a lot of strings up there."

"Thanks. I'll remember that. There's not much more Emily and I need to do, so I'm sure we'll be able to spend more time together this weekend. Thanks again, buddy."

Joe had just stepped outside the restaurant when Decker called and shocked him with the news that his father's secretary had been found dead in her apartment.

"Nash, where are you?" Decker asked—his voice filled with emotion.

"Downtown at a restaurant," Joe answered—still stunned and almost speechless with the news Michelle Rice was dead.

"Where's your sister?"

"I'm not sure. Probably at her apartment. Why?" But before Decker could answer, it hit him. "Wait! We just saw Rice a few hours ago. She told Emily she thought someone was following her."

"Apparently, someone did. Glass and I are at her apartment, and it's not pretty. Someone was trying to get information out of her. First, your father—now his secretary. What else did Rice say when you saw her?"

"I didn't talk with her. My sister did."

"We need to talk to her as soon as possible. Detective Glass called her, but she didn't answer. Can you find her?"

The detective was still talking when Joe hung up and started running towards Emily's apartment—dialing and redialing her number the whole time. His mind was racing—*had somebody been watching them at the restaurant? Did they follow his truck when he dropped Emily off?* When he reached her apartment, he started banging on the door so hard that he threatened to break the glass pane.

A yawning Emily pulled it open. "Geez, Joe, what's wrong?"

"Are you okay? Why aren't you answering your phone?"

"The battery died, and I fell asleep studying on the couch. I didn't get much sleep the other night, if you remember. Why are you trying to break my door down?"

"Decker just called. Dad's secretary has been murdered."

"God, no! What happened?"

"I don't know—but Decker's at her apartment right now. He wants us there, but my truck's back at the house. Can you drive us, and I'll let him know we're on our way?" He opened the list of recent calls on his cell and punched Decker's number.

Decker answered, and Joe said, "Detective, I've got my sister here with me." He listened for a moment. "Yes, I know exactly where it is. We'll meet you at the clubhouse in about twenty minutes." He hung up.

Michelle Rice lived at the Windjammer Apartments on Sam Rittenberg Boulevard. Decker was waiting by the clubhouse when Emily pulled up. Several police cars were lined up further inside the complex.

Joe immediately noticed a distinct change in Decker's demeanor. The antagonistic tough guy was gone. He looked shaken.

There were only a few lights on in the apartment's clubhouse. Joe and Emily sat on one of the couches, and Decker took a chair across from them.

"I've been doing this for almost thirty years," Decker said, "and this is as bad as I've ever seen."

"What do you mean?" Emily asked.

"We think whoever killed your father wanted us to believe he died of a heart attack. They simply wanted him out of the way. We think your dad knew something the killers wanted covered up. That wasn't the case here. Ms. Rice was half-naked and handcuffed. They used a knife to do things to her I don't even want to talk about."

"Oh, my God!" Emily gasped.

"So, what can we do to help?" Joe quickly asked.

Decker turned to Emily. "Your bother told us you talked with Rice. I need to know everything she told you."

Before Emily could answer, Joe jumped in, "What was the name of Dad's client that gave him all that money to invest?"

"Mr. Coldwell," she said. "Eli Coldwell. She said he owned a restaurant or bar."

Decker jotted Coldwell's name in his small notepad. "Did she tell you the name of the restaurant or bar?"

"No."

"What else did she say about this Coldwell?" Decker asked.

Emily thought for a moment and glanced at Joe. He gave a slight shake of his head. "She only mentioned that my dad worked for Mr. Coldwell for several years. He did his taxes and investments and was my dad's biggest client. I got the feeling Ms. Rice thought he was a little shady."

"Shady?" Decker questioned.

"It's just the way she talked about him. That's all," Emily said—feeling Joe didn't want her mentioning anything about drugs or prostitution.

"Okay, Ms. Nash, I want you to think about the conversation. Anything else about your father or his business?"

Joe again answered for her. "I think that was about it, Em. You told me she kept talking about how strange Dad was acting—paranoid, not sleeping. I think you said Dad was the only one who worked with Mr. Coldwell. She didn't get involved with him, right?"

Emily gave him a side glance. She wasn't sure why Joe was cutting her off.

"Right," Emily said. "She said she was scared and thought she was being followed. That was about it."

"Okay, Ms. Nash. We will follow up with Coldwell. I want you to continue to think about that conversation with Ms. Rice. Often people remember things well after the fact. We're going to be here most of the night, so please call if you think of anything else."

"I will," Emily said.

Joe started to stand, but Decker asked him to sit back down.

"There's something else. There's no way of knowing, but there's a chance that whoever murdered Ms. Rice might know you two met her today. Just be smart. What they did here took planning and patience. To be on the safe side, if you need to go out, don't go alone. Keep your doors locked and call us if you notice anything suspicious."

Emily got into her car and shot a quizzical look at Joe. "What was that all about? You kept interrupting me."

"Sorry about that, Em. But remember Rice kept on saying how Dad made her promise not to say anything about Belize. There's got to be a good reason for that, and I didn't want you to go there. I'm not saying we won't tell the detectives about it. I just want to wait to see if we can figure out why he was adamant about keeping his trips to Belize secret. That's all."

"You heard what they did to Dad's secretary," Emily said. "And there's a chance they know who we are. You told me yesterday that we would go to the police today if we didn't find out what that note meant."

"I know," Joe replied, "but just hear me out. Why would Dad give us those clues in his letter and the note on that playing card? He obviously didn't want anyone but us to figure out what it meant. Think about it. For years he was investing all that money overseas for Coldwell and his business friends. Who knows how much, but it has to be a small fortune. It may sound crazy, but I think Dad was planning on taking that money—remember how freaked out he was. I bet he did it. I bet he took that money and hid it somewhere."

"I still say we need to tell Decker," Emily said.

Joe ignored the comment. "Think about it, Em. Why would Dad go to Belize and make Rice promise not to tell anyone?"

Emily was quiet for a moment thinking the whole thing through. "I still think it's a stretch, but if you're right about everything else, then that's where the money is."

"Exactly, and that note has to be the key to finding it," Joe said. "Listen, I haven't told anyone, but I'm going to be perfectly honest with you. That $100,000 signing bonus Baltimore gave me is gone. And even if I have surgery on my elbow, there's no guarantee it'll work. Em, I'm twenty-eight, and I'm broke. And if my baseball career is over, how am I going to pay for law school? Even with a scholarship, I'm looking at around $40,000 to $50,000 a year for tuition and living expenses—and law school is three years."

"If we're being honest," Emily said, "then you need to know I've got money problems, too. When Mom and Dad got divorced, Dad set aside money for my college. Well, guess what? He used it all. There was nothing left when I started college two years ago. He'd offered to help me out a little lately, but I didn't want anything to do with him. The college gave me a good scholarship, but I still had to take out student loans. I owe about $30,000 so far, and that's not counting next semester."

"Sounds like we're both in the same boat," Joe said.

"I'm planning on using my half of what Dad left us in his will to help get me through undergraduate and graduate school."

"I wouldn't count on that," Joe said.

"What do you mean?" she said.

"Where do you think Dad got that money?" Joe asked. "Decker and Chase know Dad was murdered—and now his secretary. If they don't already know, they're going to eventually find out Coldwell and his friends were involved in drugs and other illegal stuff. They'll assume that's where Dad got the money he gave us in the will. Remember, Gallo told us all of Dad's assets are going to be frozen. We can't get that money now and probably never will."

Both of them were quiet as the reality of their situation became more apparent.

"All that may be true, but I still think we have to tell Decker about Dad's letter and the note," Emily said.

Joe could hear the hesitancy in her voice. "Let's not decide anything now. It's past 11:30. I think you should stay with me at Alex's this weekend. I know you'll feel safer there. Plus, it will give us more time to figure out what that note meant. Let's drive back to your place and get your books and a change of clothes. What do you say, Sis?"

Emily agreed, and it was well after midnight by the time they made it to Alex's house.

CHAPTER 11

EMILY AND JOE spent Saturday and Sunday together at Alex's place. Shannon stopped by Saturday morning and spent some time with them before leaving with Alex to take in a movie. Couped up in the house, Emily tried studying for her exam but couldn't shake thoughts of Michelle Rice's murder.

Joe parked himself in front of the television watching college football, but like Emily, he couldn't concentrate on the game and eventually turned off the T.V. He started padding about Alex's living room, rolling the baseball around in his hand. His thoughts kept returning to his dad's letter and the note attached to that baseball card.

He noticed Emily had put her study notes away and was staring out the window.

"Hey, Em, are you finished studying?"

"For a while, I guess," she answered.

"You know, I was thinking …"

Emily chuckled, "Well, that's promising."

"Very funny. Look it, if Dad took Coldwell's money—and I think he did—it must have been a lot, and he'd have to put it somewhere. And we both think it has to be Belize, right?"

"Right," Emily said, "and I also know someone thought Michelle Rice knew where it was and look what happened to her!"

"I know, I know," Joe said. "All I'm saying is we hold off going to the police until after the funeral on Monday. Dad wanted us to figure out the clues he gave us. If we do, I bet we find the money."

"And if we find it," Emily said, "what do we do then?"

"Let's just worry about finding it first."

Emily was about to say something when the door opened, and Alex and Shannon walked in.

"Wow," Alex said, "you guys are still here. I thought you'd be outside. It's a beautiful day. You should get out and get some fresh air."

Joe had promised himself he would tell Alex about the murders this weekend, but Shannon had been with him all day.

"Emily has her midterm exam coming up, and I was watching Georgia play Florida State."

"Well, let's have a few beers and fire-up the grill. We stopped by Publix and picked up a few steaks. Emily, it's Saturday night. No more studying. Relax, you've got all tomorrow to study."

It was an enjoyable evening. Emily did spend most of Sunday with her nose in her books, and Joe, Alex, and Shannon camped out on the couch in front of the T.V. watching the NFL games. It was late by the time Alex took Shannon back to her apartment.

The weekend had passed without further incident.

~~~~

Eli Coldwell paced back and forth in the office of his restaurant, the Blue Dolphin. He was joined by his two business associates, Michael Ferrari and Theo Jackson.

Ferrari and Jackson were polar opposites—in both physical appearance and deportment. Ferrari was small with an aggressive nature—dressing and acting like a wannabe Joe Pesci. Jackson was a large man, clean-shaven with a closely trimmed afro. He wore a gold necklace, black jeans, and a white silk T-shirt underneath a light brown leather jacket. He didn't speak often, but when he did, people listened.

"Sit the fuck down, Eli," Ferrari said. "You're making me nervous."

Coldwell reluctantly took a seat, droplets of perspiration forming on his forehead. There was no mistaking the menace in Ferrari's voice as he leaned forward and said, "Now, tell us again how you let this happen. We were under the impression that your Mr. Nash was removed from the equation."

"You know he was," Coldwell answered and shot a glance behind him at a large man leaning against the wall, his massive arms covered with tatts.

"Marvin took care of that himself."
~~~~

Marvin Simms played defensive end for the Cleveland Browns for two seasons before being arrested on a possession with intent to sell charge and spent two years in the Ohio Department of Corrections and Rehabilitation. He was neither corrected nor rehabilitated and had worked as Coldwell's strong arm for the past seven years.

Ferrari feigned a smile, his voice taking on an even more acidic tone. "So what happened? Maybe Nash's ghost emptied our account. You fucked-up big time, Coldwell. Now, what are you going to do about it?"

"I'm working on it," Coldwell replied. "We know Nash's secretary talked to his son and daughter. Plus, we know he had a lawyer named Anthony Gallo."

"I'm assuming the secretary is no longer a problem?" Jackson asked.

"She's been taken care of," Coldwell answered. "I'll get your money back. I just need some time."

"Sure, Eli. Theo and I are reasonable people. I figure forty-eight hours. That should be plenty of time." Ferrari looked at Jackson. "What do you think, Theo?"

Jackson merely stared at Coldwell as a poisonous silence filled the room before saying, "I think we're finished here." Both men stood and left without another word.

Once they were gone, Coldwell's eyes fell on Simms, and with a voice stone cold, he said, "The lawyer first."

Simms nodded and left the room.

~~~~
~~~~

Monday morning was clear with a touch of fall in the air when Joe and Emily arrived at Memorial Gardens. The cemetery covered almost 25 acres of beautifully manicured grounds—much of it covered with ancient oak trees, their large moss-covered limbs bending close to the ground. Joe parked next to the section containing their father's burial plot. A green canopy covered the gravesite.

They began walking up a gentle rise to the grave.

"Are you doing all right, Sis?"

"I'm okay. It's just … I don't know. I know we had our problems with Dad, but I'm sad he's gone."

"Yeah, I agree, but don't beat yourself up. Dad brought a lot of that on himself. At least he was trying to make amends when he wrote that letter."

Over the next 30 minutes, a few more cars pulled up—one carrying Emily's roommate, Cindy, another Alex and Shannon. Only a handful of other people showed up—Joe and Emily recognizing only a few of them. A few minutes later, everyone quietly surrounded the canopy when Joe noticed a black Cadillac Escalade pull up and park a little way off. It just remained there with no one getting out.

There was no minister to give a eulogy, but Anthony Gallo had volunteered to say a few words. Joe had to bite his tongue as he listened to Gallo describe his father as a kind person who loved his friends and family.

The actual burial service—if you could call it that—lasted no more than ten minutes.

Joe and Emily remained at the gravesite, accepting words of sympathy from a few people they'd never seen before and would never see again. After everyone left, they'd just started back to the truck when Joe noticed the Cadillac was still there.

Eli Coldwell placed a call. It was answered by Marvin Simms, who was waiting outside the cemetery gates in a 2015 dark gray Ford Focus.

"They're leaving now in a black Ford Ranger," Coldwell ordered.

Joe and Emily watched the Escalade pull away. They left the cemetery and stopped at Emily's duplex for a change of clothes and to pick up some more study material for her upcoming exam. Using a telephoto lens, Simms took several pictures of Emily and noted the address of her apartment.

A few moments after Joe parked at Alex's place, the dark gray Ford pulled over to the curb a few houses away. Simms photographed Emily and Joe and recorded Alex's Bull Street address.

After a quick lunch, Alex left for his office. Emily and Joe spent an hour or so again attempting to solve the puzzle of the letters and numbers on the note attached to the back of the playing card. Frustrated with their lack of progress, Joe dropped Emily off at her duplex. She had again planned on having a few of her classmates over that evening to study for the exam.

"Give me a call when you're finished studying, and I can bring you back here for the night," Joe suggested.

"Thanks, but I can stay here tonight. I know we'll be working really late. Don't worry, Cindy is here with me, and I promise we'll lock the doors." Emily smiled and gave Joe a peck on the cheek. "Plus, I know you and Alex will be watching Monday Night Football and don't want a girl around to bother you."

"I'll be watching the game, but Alex won't. He's out with clients tonight and won't be back till late. Just make sure to call me if you need anything."

CHAPTER 12

JOE WAS SOUND asleep when his phone woke him. It was Emily.

Still groggy, he said, "God, Em, what time is it?"

"Forget about the time, Joe!" Her excitement was unchecked. "I need you to come over here now."

"What?"

"Just get here now." She hung up.

It was 1:45 in the morning—was Emily in some sort of trouble?

He called her back, but she didn't answer. He threw on pants and a T shirt and left the house. Ten minutes later, a blurry-eyed Joe Nash arrived at Emily's apartment. She seemed okay and led him to the kitchen, where she had her computer set up.

"What is it, Em. You scared the hell out of me."

Emily just smiled at Joe for a moment before saying, "I figured it out."

"Figured what out?" Joe's patience was running thin.

"Dad's code. Well, not all of it, but here, look at this." She turned her laptop around so Joe could see the screen. "When we first got the note from the back of that playing card, I tried searching that series of letters and numbers on it." Watch this. She typed in: **NOSCBZBSXXX3736626374** and hit search.

The search screen result showed:

There are no results for NOSCBZBSXXX3736626374.

"I don't get it," Joe said.

"You will," Emily replied, obviously enjoying herself. Before Joe could say anything, she continued, "I can't believe I was so stupid. It was right there in front of me."

"I still don't get it," Joe said.

"Now, watch this." Emily entered it again, but this time she cut out the numbers, searched only with the letters.

The following appeared on the computer screen:

Swift Code (BIC) — NOSCBZBSXXX
— SCOTIABANK (BELIZE) LTD.

"Holy shit!" was all Joe could manage. "It's a damn bank account in Belize. Emily, you're amazing!"

"You're right, big brother, I am amazing. The letters are what's called a Swift Code. SWIFT is an acronym for the Society for Worldwide Interbank Financial Telecommunication. It's used to identify banks and their branches anywhere in the world. The XXX at the end means it's the main bank office."

"Now we know why Dad made those trips to Belize," Joe added. "He set up a damn bank account." Joe's excitement now matched Emily's. "And the Randy Johnson clues have to be the password."

"Exactly," Emily agreed. "Now we have the access info for Dad's secret account in Belize. What do we do now?"

"I don't know," Joe said. "I still don't even know where Belize is! And what's Usher mean? Someone who takes you to your seat?"

"I don't know either," Emily said.

"Go ahead and try to log into the account," Joe said.

Emily searched Scotiabank online but found they required a username and password—which they didn't have.

"I guess we could call the bank," Emily suggested.

"But what do we say? We don't even know for sure that it's Dad's account. It's already past 2:30. Let's call them later this morning."

"I'm sorry Joe, but I've got to take that mid-term at ten and won't get back until around noon. Plus, my brain is fried. I got to get a few hours of sleep."

"Okay," Joe said, "get some sleep and ace that test. Let me know when you're finished. Then I'll pick you up, and we can figure out what to do."

CHAPTER 13

JOE GOT LITTLE sleep—his mind consumed with Emily's revelation. *What could it mean? Whose account is it? Is it Dad's? It must have money in it, but how much?* These thoughts swirled around in his mind. And then there were the murders. *Just how safe were we?* Joe knew they should tell Decker and Glass what they knew, but now they had the SCOTIABANK account number and password. They were getting closer to what could be a bundle of money—money that would help to solve the financial problems looming for both of them.

Before he knew it, it was 6:30, shades of gray appearing through his bedroom window. He was exhausted but accepted that sleep was out of the question. He sat on the bed another minute, then decided it was time for coffee.

"Well, look who showed up." Alex was in his suit, sitting at the kitchen table, nursing a coffee. "I heard you leave in the middle of the night."

"Good morning. Just couldn't sleep." Joe poured himself a cup and joined Alex at the table. "I need to tell you something."

"About your dad?"

"Yeah." Joe paused a moment deciding how much to share. "You need to know he didn't die of a heart attack, Alex. Someone killed him."

"Jesus, Joe. I knew you were holding back something about your dad's death. I just didn't think it was anything like that."

"I'm sorry, Alex, I feel like an ass. I know I should have told you sooner. There's some stuff I still can't tell you, but you deserve to know at least some of what's going on. It gets worse. Whoever killed him also murdered his secretary. The detectives think it might be a guy named Eli Coldwell, but I think they're just as clueless as we are."

"Okay. Give me a minute here," Alex said. "That's a lot of shit to process. Are you and your sister in any danger?"

"We don't think so. Coldwell was a client of my dad. We had nothing to do with his business, but Emily and I have taken precautions anyway."

Alex told Joe to sit tight. Alex left and returned a minute later with a gun, opened a kitchen drawer, and sat it inside. "Just in case. It's a Smith & Wesson 9 millimeter semi-automatic."

"Wait a minute, Alex. I don't know anything about guns."

Alex opened the drawer and pulled it back out. "Let's take another precaution. I may have grown up in Atlanta, but my folks had a place up by the Chattanooga National Forest. I've hunted all my life." Alex brought the S&W over and showed Joe where the safety was and how to release it. "Not much to know, buddy. Just remember it's loaded." He re-engaged the safety and slid the gun back into the drawer.

Joe stared at the closed drawer. "I'm sorry, Alex. I didn't know any of this when I asked if I could stay here. This isn't fair to you or Shannon."

Alex cut him off. "Enough of that. I've got to get to work now. Keep the door locked. I should be back around five. You'll be all right. Call me if you need anything."

Alex left, and Joe locked the door behind him. He returned to the table and his coffee but found himself continuingly eyeing that drawer. *How did I get myself into this mess? My dad's dead. His secretary's dead. A secret Belize bank account. And now another gun!*

He grabbed his coffee, turned on the television in the living room, and laid down on the sofa. He eventually dozed off until his phone woke him.

"Is this Joseph Nash?"

"Yes."

"Good morning, Mr. Nash. This is Dr. Wallace from the orthopedic department at Johns Hopkins."

"Yes, doctor." Joe sat up. "I was expecting to hear from you."

"I've had a chance to review your x-rays and MRI."

Joe decided not to waste any time. "What's the verdict, doc?"

"All right, Mr. Nash, I'll get right to it. There are three bones in the elbow: the radius, the ulna, and the humerus. The ligament that connects ..."

"Excuse me, doctor," Joe interrupted. "I'm a professional baseball player. I know what the ulnar collateral ligament is. Just tell me how bad the tear is."

"I'm sorry," Wallace replied. "Of course you do. The good news is there doesn't seem to be any damage to the bones. However, the MRI did show a moderate UCL tear."

"What are the chances I can rehab without surgery?"

"That's a possibility," the doctor answered. "There've been some promising advances in physical therapy and other nonsurgical treatments."

"You don't sound too optimistic."

"Let me just say this," he began. "It's clear that your range of motion has been limited. You may recover some of that through steroid injections and intensive therapy, but to be perfectly honest, your prognosis for a complete recovery is questionable."

"The alternative is Tommy John surgery, right?"

"That's correct."

"And if I go that route," Joe said, "I'm looking at a year or more of rehab."

"Yes. The success rate is good, but, like any surgery, there are no guarantees. Rehab can be challenging, but if you stick with the program, I'd expect a complete recovery within a year-and-a-half to two years. Almost 25 percent of major league pitchers have had the surgery at some point."

"I know," Joe said. "I respect your opinion, doc. I just need some time to sort through this."

"Of course. And good luck with whatever decision you make."

Joe disconnected the call. "Shit." He'd been expecting this—he just didn't want to admit it to himself. He'd come so close to his dream. *This isn't fucking fair!* He was about to turn twenty-eight, and now he'd be looking at maybe two more years before he could get back. *Hell, by then, I'll be pushing thirty.*

His thoughts swung back to Belize. There was no getting around the fact that if his baseball career were over, he would have significant money problems. And with two more years of undergraduate and another two of graduate school, Emily was facing the same situation. It was clear to him his Dad wanted them to have whatever money was in that account—even though it was from questionable sources. If they got caught, they could be in some serious legal trouble. But it wouldn't hurt to at least call the bank and find out where they stood.

Since the funeral, Joe's mind continued to shift back to the cemetery and Eli Coldwell's black Escalade. He got off the couch and looked out of the living room window—fully expecting to see the Cadillac. It wasn't there. He shook his head and smiled to himself before heading to the bathroom, where he showered and shaved. He got dressed and returned to the living room to wait for Emily's phone call.

He didn't have to wait long. Ten minutes later, Emily called, letting Joe know she'd finished her exam.

"You should have called me this morning. I would have taken you to your class."

"No problem. Cindy's boyfriend spent the night, and he walked us to campus this morning."

"How did you do on your test?" Joe asked.

"Good, I think. I'm leaving in a few minutes. Do you want to meet at my apartment?"

"You're at the Math & Science Building, right?"

"Right."

"Stay there, and I'll come and get you. We can come back here and call Belize."

He picked up Emily and was back at the house about twenty minutes later.

"How do you want to handle this?" Joe asked.

She pulled a note from her pocket and handed it to him. "Here's the bank's phone number and the account number. I also put the numbers you got from those Randy Johnson words. I thought you could call and say you have some questions about your account number."

Joe removed his cell. "I suppose that's as good as anything—even though we're not sure whose account this really is. All set?"

Emily nodded, and Joe dialed the number. It was answered immediately. He mentioned he had a question about his account and read off the numbers.

"Certainly, sir. And who may I say is calling?"

"Mr. Nash," Joe replied, intentionally omitting his first name.

"Please hold." Joe waited almost a full minute before she returned to the phone. "I have Mr. Usher on the other line. I can connect you now."

There was a click, and a voice said, "This is Clinton Usher."

Usher? Joe thought. *So Usher is the banker!* He waited, but the man said nothing else. He had Emily's note in front of him and said he had some questions about the account.

"And the access code, sir?"

"1988-2009-51."

"Thank you, Mr. Nash. Is your sister there with you?"

"Yes," Joe answered—surprised Usher mentioned Emily.

"Good." He then explained that the account stipulated that a new password would be issued once the contact had been made and verified. One of the bank's U.S. attorneys by the name of James Bellamy would be in contact with him to review the contents of the account and, at that time, pass on the new password. He also related that both he and his sister must be present for the account contents and password to be revealed.

"Mr. Bellamy will be your liaison for any further dealings with our bank. It was a pleasure speaking with you, Mr. Nash." Usher ended the phone call.

"What did they say?" Emily asked.

Joe looked dumbfounded. "That was Mr. Usher."

Emily's eyes popped wide open. "Usher? You got to be kidding me! What did he say?"

Joe passed on the information Usher had given him about James Bellamy and that a new password would be issued for the account.

"When will Bellamy contact us?" Emily asked.

"Usher said in the next few days."

"Well, that's great. At least now we know what Dad meant by 'Usher,' but we still don't know what the hell's going on. This is crazy."

~~~~

Marvin Simms sat in an older dark green Chevy Blazer, eyeing the light emanating from Gallo's second-floor office window. The Blazer had been stolen the night before from a house on the outskirts of Goose Creek.

Shortly after six, a few lights flicked off in Gallo's reception room, and a woman walked out and entered a car parked immediately outside the building. As the car drove away, Simms pulled a stocking over his head and adjusted his black ball cap low over his face.

Gallo remained in his office—his suit jacket off and tie loosened. A slew of legal documents covered his desk.

Simms entered the building, removed the stocking and ball cap, and quietly scaled the staircase. At the top, he turned the knob on the office door. It was locked. He removed a small leather case and used a titanium feeder pick and tension tool to release the door lock quietly.
~~~~

A few tiffany lamps remained lit, casting shadows on the walls inside the reception room. A partially opened door leaked light from the hallway leading to Gallo's office. Simms stealthily proceeded down the hallway, stopping outside Gallo's cracked door.

He removed a black cylinder from his packet and eased the door open. Gallo looked up and was startled to see a large man moving quickly toward him. He stood, knocking over his chair. Simms extended a gloved hand and pressed a trigger, breaking open a compressed-nitrogen cartridge that sent two wired darts into Gallo's chest. He screamed as a high voltage current made his body convulse, sending him crashing into his credenza. Simms was on him a second later. A vicious punch to the side of his head sent him tumbling to the floor, rendering him unconscious. Simms slapped a pair of handcuffs on Gallo and lifted his body back up onto his chair. He tore off a portion of thick gray tape and placed it over Gallo's mouth.

A moment later, Gallo began moaning. He shook his head back and forth, his moans growing louder. Simms slapped him across his face. "Shut the fuck up and listen to me. I have questions for you. Answer them, and you won't get hurt."

Simms yanked out the darts and tore off the tape. Gallo's eyes widened when the big man removed a knife and snapped open its six-inch blade.

"Where did Nash send the money?"

Still in pain, Gallo managed, "I don't know what you're talking about."

"Wrong answer." The knife flashed forward, slicing off a small portion of Gallo's left ear.

"Where did Nash send the money?" Simms calmly repeated.

Blood running down his neck, he pleaded, "Jesus Christ! I don't know!"

"Wrong answer." The knife found Gallo's left shoulder—opening a five-inch gash and turning his white shirt sleeve ruby red. "We know you talked to his kids." Simms inserted the blade into Gallo's left nostril. "Do they know where the money is?"

"For God's sake, I don't know. Nash made me promise to give them a letter if he died. I did. That's all. I promise!"

A flick of the wrist and the knife opened Gallo's nose. "What's in the letter?"

Gallo shut his eyes, clenched his teeth, and moaned, "I don't know. I swear I never saw it. I gave it to his son and daughter."

"Wrong answer." Simms slit open Gallo's throat and quickly backed away, watching Gallo's life drain away.

He put the stocking and cap back on and quickly exited. The stolen Blazer ended up behind an abandoned barn where Simms had parked his Focus earlier that day.

Later that night, Simms showed up at the Blue Dolphin.

Coldwell let him in his office, and before even closing the door, asked, "Did you find the money?"

"I don't think the lawyer knew anything about it," Simms said. "But I get the feeling Nash's kids might. The guy said he gave them some sort of secret letter."

"You took care of the lawyer, right?"

"Of course."

"Well, we know where those kids are," Coldwell growled. "Find the fucking letter!"

CHAPTER 14

THE FOLLOWING MORNING, Arlene Hanson had the office key out and was about to open up the law office when she noticed the door was slightly ajar, but most of the reception room lights were still off. Curious, she entered.

"Anthony, are you in here?"

No answer. The hallway door was open, and she could see light coming from Gallo's office. Approaching the door, she called out, "Did you know the front door was …" She froze when she saw Gallo's milk-white face and blood-soaked body sprawled across his chair. She screamed and stumbled backward—dropping her purse as she ran down the stairs.

She burst from the building, almost knocking into an older man on the sidewalk. Shaking, she screamed, "Oh, God. Help. Please help!"

The man backed away, but she grabbed him. "Please! Help! He's dead!"

"What are you talking about?"

"Anthony! It's Anthony! Please! Call someone!"

Recovering from his initial shock, the man pulled out his phone and dialed 9-1-1.

~~~~

Detective Decker was in Captain Adam Stone's office at Lockwood. Stone ran the Drug Strike Force and was responsible for coordinating all undercover investigations with the FBI, DEA, and Homeland Security.

"Captain, what can you tell me about Eli Coldwell?" Decker asked.

"Coldwell's a small-time hood running some low-level drug and prostitution rackets for the mob. He operates mostly within Charleston County. DEA and FBI haven't paid much attention to him—they've got bigger fish to fry. He's on our radar, though. He may be small-time, but that's not to say he isn't dangerous—especially because he's connected at the hip with Michael Ferrari and Theo Jackson. Those two have crews working the same game. They operate mostly in North Charleston. What's up with Coldwell?"

"We think he's involved in the murders of Frank Nash and his secretary."

"What makes you think that?"

"Nash managed a lot of Coldwell's money, mostly international stuff. We've got Nash's computers, but the accounts
~~~~

are encrypted, and our computer techs haven't been able to crack them."

"That's all you got?" Stone responded. "Sounds pretty thin."

"That's it, so far."

"Any other suspects?"

"Not yet. But I'd like to bring Coldwell in for questioning."

"I can help with that," Stone said. "One of my detectives is assigned to keep tabs on him. We've been monitoring the operations of all three of those assholes. We've busted their hookers and harassed their street pushers but haven't been able to come up with enough to put them away." Stone made the call and instructed the detective to bring in Coldwell.

"When do you think he can get him in here?" Decker asked. But before Stone could answer, there was a knock.

"Come in," Stone called out.

Detective Glass opened the door—a distressed look on his face. "We got another one. Nash's lawyer was just found dead in his office. I've got officers on their way there now."

"Shit," Decker said, "that's the third."

"All right," Stone said, "get the hell out there, and let me know what you've got."

Decker stood and started for the door but stopped and asked, "Justin, what about Nash's kids? Do they know yet?"

"I don't know," Glass snapped. "I just got the call myself." He regained his composure. "I'll get officers to chase them down."

"When they find them, tell our boys to sit on them. They may be next."

~~~~

A few minutes later, the detectives were on their way to Daniel Island. Glass tried Emily's cell a few times without luck. But he was able to get ahold of Joe.

"Mr. Nash, this is Detective Glass. Where are you now?"

"At my friend's place, where I've been staying. Why?"

"We have officers on their way there now. I'm afraid there's been another murder, your father's attorney, Anthony Gallo."

"Jesus! We just met with him last week. What happened?"

"Not sure. I'm on my way there now. Do you know where your sister is?"

"I imagine she's in class or on her way."

"We've called her cell, and she didn't answer. Do you know where her class is?"

"It's a computer class. All those are in the Math & Science Building."

Glass started to say he would send his officer there when Joe hung up, grabbed his windbreaker, and was out the door for the Math & Science Building. He was pissed at himself for not insisting she spend the night with him at Alex's.

As soon as he made it to the building, he caught someone in the hall and found the classroom. He knocked on the door,
~~~~

and a professor opened it. He was about to say something when Joe blurted, "Is Emily Nash here?"

"I'm in the middle of a class," the professor protested.

Joe pushed past him and looked inside. There were only about ten students, and Emily was not one of them. He turned back to the professor. "Did Emily show up this morning?"

"She did not, and you're interrupting my ..." Joe was gone before he heard the rest.

He called Glass. "She's not in her class!"

"Stay there," Glass ordered. "I'll have my officers pick you up."

~~~~

Two police cars were outside Gallo's building when Decker and Glass arrived. Two officers were standing by a squad car, speaking with a man and a woman; a third officer stood sentinel at the door to the building. When the detectives approached, he moved aside and said, "Upstairs."

Another officer was stationed at the top of the stairs outside the office. He pointed. "First door down the hall on the right."

After slipping on plastic gloves, the two made their way into Gallo's office.

"Jesus," Glass whispered.

The blood covering Gallo's face and chest, as well as the arterial spray across his desk, had congealed to a dark rust red. His face had taken on a ghostly pallor, and his lifeless eyes
~~~~

stared straight ahead. His mouth was agape. A few flies had already found the open crevasse in his neck.

Taking care not to step in blood, Decker moved forward. He noticed the handcuffs.

"Cuffed, just like Rice. Whoever did this was looking for information. And I don't doubt they got it."

"Sick son-of-a-bitch," Glass mumbled.

Hearing footsteps, they both turned and saw Alice O'Sullivan.

"Good morning, detectives. A lovely way to start the day, don't you think?"

Taking in the scene, she moved to the body and began scrutinizing its condition. Using a pen, she raised the cuff on one of Gallo's pant legs, exposing the skin. The deep blue indicated advanced lividity. She carefully attempted to move Gallo's cuffed hands and, almost to herself, said, "Complete rigor. Dead at least twelve hours." She inspected the partially severed throat. "Clean cut. No serrations on the knife—probably a switchblade or the like. Ear, nose, and arm incisions were intended to cause pain. There was some intense persuasion going on here, gentlemen."

~~~~

Joe paced outside the Math & Science Building, waiting for the officers. A few minutes later, the squad car pulled up, and an officer got out. Joe ran to the car.

"Mr. Nash?" the officer questioned.
~~~~

Joe nodded and blurted, "I can't find my sister!"

"We know, sir." He opened the rear door. "We've been ordered to take you back to the station."

"I'm not going to any station. Take me to my sister's apartment."

The officers conferred. "Okay, but we'll need to stay with you."

"I don't care. Drive down Comings Street. That's the way she would have walked. Go!"

They made a U-turn and drove down Comings. Joe scanned both sides of the street, but Emily was nowhere in sight. As they pulled up to her duplex, Joe jumped out before they came to a stop. One officer removed his gun, grabbed Joe's arm, and ordered, "Get behind us!" The officers stationed themselves on either side of the door and knocked—no answer. They called out, "Police! Open the door! Police!" They entered and, seeing the living room and kitchen empty, fanned out to clear the bedrooms.

Just as one officer reported his bedroom was clear, the other called out, "She's in here!"

Cindy was spread-eagle on the bed—her hands and feet made fast to the bedposts with black zip ties, and her mouth taped shut. Her face was bloodied, her eyes wide open and frantic. Joe followed the officer into the bedroom just as his partner was removing the tape. "You're going to be okay, miss."

Cindy began to cry. Joe approached and said, "Where's Emily?"

"Two of them. There were two of them."

"Where's Emily?" Joe repeated.

"I don't know!" Cindy sobbed. "I couldn't do anything. I'm sorry."

Joe took Cindy's hand. "Tell me what happened."

"I was asleep when I heard something. I looked at my alarm, and it was after three in the morning. I was getting out of bed when two men ran in. Something hit me, and when I woke up, I was tied up. I'm sorry."

One officer finished cutting the ties and asked, "Did you see their faces?"

Despite what she'd been through, she was apologetic. "No. I'm sorry. It was too dark."

The other officer was on his phone with Detective Glass, describing what they'd found. "Yes, sir," the officer said and turned to Joe. "Mr. Nash, Detective Glass wants to speak with you."

Joe grabbed the phone. "They've got my sister!"

The detective's voice took on an authoritative tone. "Mr. Nash, I need you to calm down. Listen to me carefully. We're going to get you to Lockwood. I'll meet you there. We're on this. Now, let me talk to the officer." Joe was flustered but handed the phone back to the officer. "Additional officers, forensics, and EMS have been dispatched. I want you to remain at the scene and have your partner take Nash to the station and make sure he stays there."

Glass hung up and advised Decker what had happened at Emily's apartment.

Decker looked at his watch. "All right, I'll stay here until we get things coordinated. Then I want another crack at Nash. Outside of Coldwell, we've got nothing. No evidence trail, no murder weapon, no prints—nothing. We've got no traction on the case. We need a break, and I'm convinced Nash and his sister know more than they're telling us. Their father, his secretary, and now the lawyer—all murdered. Those kids know something, and I intend to find out what it is."

CHAPTER 15

JOE HAD BEEN in a small conference room at Lockwood for almost an hour before Decker walked in. Joe looked like a caged animal. "What's going on? No one's telling me a damn thing!"

"Please, sit down, Mr. Nash. I'll tell you what we're doing so far." Joe reluctantly sat, and Decker continued, "We have forensics at your sister's apartment. Hopefully, they'll find something helpful. We know the attack occurred at approximately three in the morning. Unfortunately, your sister's roommate wasn't able to identify her attackers."

"I know all that!" Joe shot back.

Decker remained calm. "I'm afraid we have to assume that whoever did this has taken your sister. We're checking to see if any security cameras are in the area. We'll also have officers canvass neighbors to see if anyone saw something."

Joe slumped in his chair, head turned away, gaze in the middle distance. He had a sober look about him. "It's my fault. I should have known something like …" His voice faded. He turned back and focused on Decker. "What happens now?"

"We wait," Decker said.

"Wait for what?"

"We have to assume whoever did this is convinced you and your sister know something—something that they're desperate to find out. And if they don't get what they need from your sister, they'll call you."

Joe again turned his head away.

"Nash, look at me." Decker's voice was firm but understanding. "We're bringing Eli Coldwell in for questioning. Give me something to work with. We know there are things you haven't told us. Someone has your sister, Nash. And I think you know what they want and what they'll do to get it. Whatever it is, is it worth your sister's life?"

Is it worth your sister's life?

It was a gut punch. He'd gotten caught up in the cloak of mystery surrounding their father's letter. It had become almost a game —follow the clues and find the treasure. Even after Rice was murdered, he still turned a blind eye to the possible dangers of continuing to play the game. He was so naive. Now Emily's life hung in the balance. *Enough! All this has to end!*

Finally, Joe nodded his head and looked directly at Decker. "It's the money, detective."

Decker removed his cell, punched the record icon, and leaned forward. "Go ahead. Tell me about the money."

Joe let it all out—everything. The meeting with Gallo, the letter, the note on the baseball card, the offshore account, the call to the SCOTIABANK in Belize, Mr. Usher.

"Does your sister know all this?"

"Yes, she knows all of it." Then suddenly, Joe's head snapped up. "Wait! There's something else. Usher told us he had instructions from my dad to change the password as soon as he was contacted about the account. A lawyer from the bank is supposed to meet us, explain everything, and give us the new password. That means nothing can happen with that Belize account until I talk to the lawyer."

"When is this lawyer supposed to meet you?"

"I don't know. Usher never said, but I would think soon."

An officer stuck his head into the conference room. "Sir, Mr. Coldwell is in Conference Room 2."

"Thanks, I'll be there in a minute." He turned back to Joe. "I want you to wait here. This won't take long."

~~~~

Coldwell sat in a metal chair, legs crossed, looking surprisingly comfortable amid the grim surroundings. A moment later, Detective Decker entered and introduced himself.

"Hello, detective. I have to admit I was a bit surprised when one of your cohorts brought me in here. I assume it's because I knew Frank Nash. Is that correct, detective?"
~~~~

"Right. We understand you were one of Mr. Nash's biggest clients. I imagine you knew him well. We're hoping you can help us with our investigation into his death."

"Yes, such a sad thing," Coldwell said, as if in passing. "I knew him, but only in a business sense. However, we did share a love for the game of baseball. Actually, I met him at a College of Charleston baseball luncheon. He did indeed do some investing for me the last few years, but to tell you the truth, he wasn't all that good at it. I lost a fair amount of money in the first year or two. I didn't do much with him after that."

"We heard Mr. Nash specialized in the international market," Decker said. "I'm assuming that's where your funds were invested."

"I imagine so," Coldwell replied, "but I didn't pay all that much attention. You know we're not talking about a lot of money here."

"And just how much money are we talking about, Mr. Coldwell?"

"I'm not entirely sure—perhaps around $40,000. Why all the questions, detective? I told you I didn't know him well."

Hoping to catch Coldwell off guard, Decker changed the subject. "How about Michael Ferrari and Theo Jackson? Do you know if they invested with Frank Nash?"

"I wouldn't know, detective."

"How about last Friday evening?" Decker pushed. "Where were you?"

"And why do you want to know?" Coldwell answered. He knew where this was going.

"Just answer the question, Mr. Coldwell."

"Are you insinuating I had something to do with Frank Nash's death? Am I being interrogated?"

Decker leaned forward. "I was under the impression you were Mr. Nash's main client. You said $40,000—that doesn't seem like much of an investment to put in an offshore account. Are you sure that's all you gave him?"

"What does that have to do with your investigation?"

"It's just a simple question," Decker pressed. "There are some rough edges in the case. Just trying to smooth them out, that's all. How about last Friday night? Where were you?"

Coldwell stood. "I think we're done here. But if you must know, last Friday I was at my restaurant, the Blue Dolphin, from around three in the afternoon until closing. I'm there almost every night."

He started toward the door. "I'll have an officer escort you out," Decker said. He opened the door and called out to the bullpen. "Chuck, do me a favor and show Mr. Coldwell where the front door is." He looked back at Coldwell. "You have a nice day, sir. I'm sure we'll be talking again."

Decker watched him go and then returned to the other conference room.

As he walked in, Joe said, "What do you think? What happened? Did you get anything about Emily?"

"No, but it's clear to me that Coldwell is involved. The problem is we've got no hard evidence, so we can't hold him."

"What about his bank account. Can't you get a warrant or something?"

"First of all," Decker replied, "we don't have enough for a judge to issue a warrant. Even if we did, the kind of money we're talking about would never see the inside of a bank."

Joe looked puzzled. "What do you mean?"

"Coldwell and two of his associates are involved in criminal activities—the kind of activities that generate cash, and that requires money laundering or at least a good place to hide it."

"So if he's a criminal, what are you going to do about it?"

"All right, here's where we are—my partner's at Gallo's office. I'm sure forensics is working the scene. But because we've discovered very little from the other two crime scenes, I doubt they'll find much. It seems clear we're dealing with a professional. Coldwell invested money with your father. We know your father was most likely the one who moved that money into the Belize account. Rice or Gallo must have told the murderer about you and your sister. They targeted your sister to find out where their money went."

"Maybe she wouldn't tell them."

"Mr. Nash, you need to understand that whoever has your sister will get that information—one way or the other. The question is, would your sister remember the account number and original password?"

"Maybe the password," Joe said. "I don't know about the account number. Probably not."

"Even if she does remember, it sounds like the bank has already issued a new password," Decker added. "The account number is worthless without that."

It was now clear to Joe. "That's why they're going to have to contact me, right?"

"Yes, and we need to be ready for that. I already have officers on standby. If and when they call, we can track the location of the phone—whether it's a landline, regular cell, or even a burner phone."

"How long does it take? I mean, how long do I have to keep them on the line?"

"Don't worry about that. We can get locations almost immediately. If the call comes from a landline, we'll know the exact location of the phone. It's not quite as specific if it's a cell—we'll get the cell towers and triangulate the location. Identifying a specific location depends on the number and proximity of towers. For example, downtown, we can often narrow phones within a radius of a hundred feet. As the phone moves away from concentrated population centers, there are fewer towers, and it gets a little trickier."

"So that means I have to stay here?" Joe asked.

"Yes, we'll set everything up right here in the conference room. Almost all kidnappers contact the families with their demands by phone. We'll be listening and recording any call you receive. Sit tight for a minute. I'll be right back." Decker left and returned a moment later with a man carrying a small bin full of wires and connectors. "Mr. Nash, this is Tech Officer Osborne. He'll be working the phone trace."

Joe looked at the bin and wires.

"We call that the Octopus," Decker said. "Give me your cell." Joe passed it over, and Decker connected a wire to the phone's earphone dock. The other end of the five-foot wire went into a small black box. Several additional cables came out of the box, each extending another five feet. Decker removed two headphones and a digital recorder from the bin and connected them to the remaining wires. "The Octopus allows us to listen, record, and trace."

"So you're saying I'm going to have to stay here until whoever has Emily calls?"

"Yes," Decker answered and looked at his watch. "I'm sure they're watching where you were staying. It's not safe going back there. If they can't find you, trust me, they'll call your cell phone."

Decker left the room, returning with a large canister of coffee, cream and sugar, several Styrofoam cups, and a box filled with a half dozen donuts. "Make yourself as comfortable as you can."

Joe was pouring himself a cup when the door opened, and Detective Glass entered. He nodded at Joe and turned to Decker. "Anyone call?"

"No," Decker said. "Tell me about the lawyer."

Glass gave a brief rundown of what transpired at Gallo's office. He finished by saying, "I'm not sure how much we'll get, Max."

Joe, Decker, Glass, and the technician settled in to wait for what they hoped would be the kidnapper's call.

A good hour had passed when Joe asked why he hadn't received the call yet.

"First of all," Decker explained, "they've probably tried to find you at your friend's house where you were staying. They will also hold off calling, knowing you'll get more nervous the longer you hear nothing about your sister. I know it's hard but try to be patient. They will call."

Joe became increasingly despondent as the hours dragged on.

CHAPTER 16

AROUND FOUR O'CLOCK, there was a knock on the door, and a forensic computer tech named Steve Gagyi entered with a laptop and printout.

"Detectives, I have something." He walked over and laid the printout in front of Decker and Glass. "As you know, we've been working on the computers from Mr. Nash's office. The form of encryption used on Coldwell's international files was complex, but we finally broke it." He pointed to the top of the printout. "This is a listing of the international transfers Nash made for his clients over the past several years."

Decker bent forward, studying the sheet. "I don't get it. There are dates but no dollar amounts."

"Correct but look at the amounts for Mr. Coldwell's account." Gagyi flipped to the last sheet. "All the amounts are deleted but take a look at the bottom here."

WPACKYXXXX583473997756
8YOGIBERRA1965
$10,245,756

Gagyi continued, "The letters in the top three lines are designations for Westpac Bank in the Grand Cayman Islands. It's used when money is wired. The twelve numbers following the letters identify the specific account at the bank. I assume the second series of numbers and letters is a password for the account. And it seems apparent that Mr. Nash had accumulated over $10 million in Mr. Coldwell's Cayman Islands account."

Joe had to smile. "Yogi Berra! My Dad's favorite player. His number was 8, he retired in 1965."

Glass looked at Decker. "What do you think, Max? Is this enough for an arrest warrant?"

"It's a stretch, but it's worth a try. I'm convinced Coldwell is behind these murders, but everything we've got is circumstantial. Plus, there's no way we can move on him while the girl's being held hostage. Go ahead and write the warrant and get it to Judge Roberts. We'll eventually need it."

Joe sat there thinking to himself, *Where could my sister be? What are they doing to her?*

Gagyi had been sitting quietly, taking in everything. He waited until Decker finished talking before saying, "Excuse me, sir. Nash was a CPA. While my team was attempting to break his encrypted files, we discovered that in addition to investing Coldwell's money, he also prepared tax returns for his restaurant."

"We know he did Coldwell's taxes," Decker said dismissively.

Gagyi disregarded his comment and continued, "We found a warehouse listed in his assets and liabilities statement. It's at 35 Hipp Street, close to the Navy Shipyards."

The significance of Gagyi's discovery was immediately apparent to everyone in the room.

"Show me the warehouse on Google Earth," Decker said.

Gagyi pulled it up and focused on the warehouse and its surroundings. It was a small building located well off the street with six or seven parking spaces in the rear.

"Maybe he's got Emily there!" Joe exuded.

Decker was about to say something when Joe's cell rang. Everyone froze. Osborne activated the digital recorder and slipped on his earphones. Decker did the same, nodded, and pointed at Joe.

Alex Cooper's name appeared on Joe's cell. "Alex?"

"Hey, Joe. Just checking in to see if everything's okay. I'm getting off early, and I thought I'd pick up a pizza on the way home."

Joe put his hand over his cell. "It's my friend, Alex Cooper."

Decker shook his head and signaled for Joe to cut the call.

Joe ignored him. "Alex, listen to me. Something's happened. My Dad's lawyer was just killed, and it looks like whoever did it has Emily."

"What do you mean someone has Emily? She's been kidnapped?"

"Yeah, I'm at the police station. They think whoever has her is going to call me."

"What can I do?" Alex asked—his voice filled with concern.

"There is something," Joe said. "I can't believe I forgot about it. My backpack—I need some things in there. Can you bring it to the Lockwood police station?"

"I'm leaving right now," Alex said. "I'll be there as soon as I can."

CHAPTER 17

"WHAT'S IN YOUR pack?" Decker asked.

"The letter from my Dad and the note from the baseball card with the Belize account number and password I told you about. If they call, they're going to want those."

"Right," Decker affirmed—mad at himself he hadn't thought of that before now.

"What about that warehouse?" Joe asked. "Could they have Emily there?"

"Possibly," Decker answered. "I'll have officers stationed there to covertly monitor the building."

It took Alex almost a half hour to get to his house, find the backpack, and make it to Lockwood. As soon as Alex walked into the conference room, Joe was on his feet. Alex gave Joe his pack, and the two hugged. Joe felt an overwhelming sense of relief now that his friend was with him.

Decker thanked Alex and ordered him out.

"Wait," Joe said, "I want him to stay." He then turned to Alex. "That is if you'll do it."

"Of course," Alex answered without hesitation.

Decker was visibly agitated. "Mr. Nash, I'm going to insist that—"

"He stays! He's my friend, and I say he stays."

Not used to being challenged by a civilian, Decker was about to again insist Alex leave when Joe spoke up, "Look, detective, it's important to me he stays. He knows about the murders and Coldwell. I know he won't do anything to get in the way of what you're doing here."

Decker was still fuming, and after a moment, he said, "Okay, but he stays out of the way and keeps his mouth shut. If he doesn't, he's out. Is that understood?"

Both Joe and Alex nodded their agreement.

Everyone again settled in to wait for what they expected would be the kidnapper's call. Gagyi left to go to his office, Decker spent most of this time on his phone, and Joe and Alex huddled together in constant conversation.

The afternoon hours dragged on until about five when Joe's cell rang.

"Wait!" Decker said. "When they ask, tell them you can't remember the account number, but you can get it. That will buy us more time."

Decker scrambled to put his headphones on, and the technician nodded to Joe.

"Hello."

"Mr. Nash." The voice was muffled, digitally modified to hide the speaker's identity.

"Where's my sister?"

"Your sister is safe. But if you want her to stay safe, we need some information."

"What? What do you want?"

"Your sister was kind enough to tell us about the Scotiabank account in Belize. You know what we want—the account number and password."

"I don't have them with me." Joe paused. "But I can get them."

There was a pause on the other end. "I'm not a patient man, Mr. Nash. I will call you back in exactly one hour. Oh, and by the way, if we find out you have contacted the police, there will be consequences." The call was disconnected.

Decker looked at Officer Osborne. "Did you get it?"

"Yes. Off Calhoun, about halfway between King and Meeting. Right next to Marion Square."

Decker called dispatch and gave the location and instructions for two unmarked squad cars to proceed with all due haste but not to intercede.

"What happens now?" Joe asked.

"Officers are on their way."

"Wait! You heard what he said. If they know I'm with the police, they'll hurt Emily."

"Trust me, Nash. As long as they don't have the account information, nothing will happen to your sister."

It was a matter of minutes before Decker's phone rang. He answered and listened intently before muttering, "Shit." He hung up. "They found a smashed burner phone with its SIM card removed."

"How about security cameras?" Joe asked.

"We'll check, but big oak trees and dense foliage cover most of those walkways. It'll be tough picking anything up."

"So what's next?"

Decker looked at his watch. "We've got about fifty minutes until the next call. Before you give the account information, insist you talk to your sister to make sure she's okay. Whoever calls may not be where they're holding her. They'll threaten you. They'll say your sister will be hurt if you don't tell them. Be calm but tell them you won't give them anything until you talk to her."

Joe was tired of Decker referring to Emily as "your sister"—like she was a pawn in a chess game. "Okay, I'll do it. And by the way, my sister has a name—Emily."

"Right, Emily," Decker said and quickly continued, "That will buy us a little more time. If we're lucky, we might even be able to identify where she's being held."

Decker called Captain Stone with an update. "Captain, if Coldwell's not already at his restaurant, he'll be there shortly. We also know he has a small warehouse by the Navy Shipyards. There's a good chance he has Nash's sister there. We're awaiting another call from the kidnappers."

"What do you need, Max?"

"Justin is writing up an arrest warrant for Coldwell. If we get it, he can take a group of officers out to Coldwell's restaurant. Even if we don't get it, we can bring him in and detain him for questioning. I have officers monitoring the warehouse but would like to have SWAT ready if we need to move on it."

"I'll have Chito get his people ready and tell him you'll be calling with the specifics."

"Thanks, Captain. I'll keep you up to date on what's happening."

While Decker was on his cell, Alex, who had been silent, sat down next to Joe. "How are you holding up, buddy?"

"Not so good. I should have known something like this would happen. I screwed up big time, Alex."

Alex put his hand on Joe's shoulder. "Anything I can do?"

"No," Joe's voice began to break. "Just stick with me."

Time stood still as they waited for the next call. Decker was strategizing with Chito Walker when Joe's cell rang. "Chito, I'll call you back."

Osborne checked his monitor and nodded.

"Go ahead," Decker said. "Pick it up. Remember no information until you talk to your sister."

Joe answered his phone. "Is Emily there? I need to talk to her."

"Okay," the modified voice said. "Then I get the account number and password, or you'll never talk to her again. Do you understand?"

"Yes, put her on."

There was a short pause. The voice modifier was switched off, and Emily came on the line—her familiar voice sounded confused.

"Joe?"

"Em, are you all right? Did they hurt you?"

"I feel tired—kinda out of it. I think they gave me something. But I'm okay. There's something over my head. I can't see anything."

"But they haven't hurt you, right?"

"No, I don't think so."

Another pause and the altered voice returned. "Now, Mr. Nash, the information?"

Joe referred to the paper in front of him. "You need to know something before you hang up."

"The account number and password, Mr. Nash. I said give them to me!"

Joe slowly read the account number and password. He was asked to repeat them, and he did. As soon as he finished, he added, "Don't hang up. You need to know something. The password has been changed. I didn't do it. The bank did. They haven't given me the new one yet but will any time now. I promise I can get it—just don't hurt my sister!"

The line went dead.

"Shit!" Decker shouted. He looked at Osborne. "Did you get it?"

"The call kept pinging off different towers," Osborne said. "Whoever was calling was moving. They were on King Street when I lost them."

"God damn it!" Joe said. "What are we supposed to do now! They've got Emily."

"They're not going to hurt your sister, Nash," Decker said. "They need that new password. We just sit tight."

"Wait a second!" Joe opened his cell and checked his recent outgoing calls. He found the number he had dialed back when he and Emily had first called the bank: 011-501-227-2707.

Joe placed the call, and it was answered almost immediately. "Hello, this is Joe Nash. I need to talk to Mr. Usher."

"Please hold the line, Mr. Nash."

The operator was back a moment later. "I'm sorry, Mr. Nash. Mr. Usher is in a meeting. May I take your number?"

"Tell him it's an emergency. He'll talk to me."

"Hold on, please."

After a short hold, Usher was on the line. "Mr. Nash, what can I do for you?"

"I need the new password to my father's account. Now."

"I told your sister our attorney will contact you."

"You don't understand." Joe's voice was firm as he explained that Emily had been taken and what the kidnappers were demanding.

There was a pause before Usher answered, "Your father warned me there may be some issues with the account. He made several prerequisite requirements—some dealing with how the account, or a portion of it, can be transferred. One stipulation is that any account information must be given to you or your sister personally by a bank representative. I appreciate this is frustrating, but we must be guided by his wishes."

"I just told you she's been taken!" Joe's voice grew louder. "I don't have time!"

"I understand, Mr. Nash. I do not personally know the new password. Only Mr. Bellamy has it, but I know he is to arrive in Charleston this evening. I will contact him now and explain your situation. He should be calling you shortly."

"Okay," Joe said. "Please hurry!"

Decker had been listening to Joe. "What did he say?"

"He's going to get ahold of their U.S. lawyer and have him call me."

As if on cue, Joe's cell rang again.

"Wait!" Decker ordered. "If that's the kidnappers, tell them the bank will be getting you the new password this evening. You just need more time."

Joe answered the call.

"This is your last chance, Nash. We need that password, or your sister dies. It's as simple as that."

"I told you they're giving me the password this evening! I promise I'll give it to you. Just don't do anything to my sister! Please!"

"Do whatever you need to do. You have three hours. That's it. We get that password, or you'll never see your sister again."

The call disconnected.

A hush fell over the group. No one spoke. It was 6:30. They would get the final call at 9:30 that night. Emily's life hung in the balance.

Finally, Decker tore off his earphones. "Damn it!"

CHAPTER 18

THE GROUP LISTENED in anticipation as Joe explained Usher told him that SCOTIABANK'S U.S. attorney was on his way to Charleston and would be calling him shortly. He was the only person who possessed the new password.

"Okay, hopefully, we'll get that password shortly," Decker said. "Chito will have his SWAT boys deployed around Coldwell's warehouse, and Justin will have officers ready to move on his restaurant."

A few minutes later, Joe got the lawyer's call.

He answered and listened for a moment before he raised his voice and said, "No, I don't think *you* understand. My sister's life is in danger! She's been kidnapped!" He listened another moment. "I don't give a damn about that." He listened further. "All right, I'll meet you there." The whole call lasted less than thirty seconds. Joe hung up and felt like throwing his phone.

"What did he say?" Decker asked.

"His name is Bellamy, and he's at the Atlanta Airport. He said he was in the process of boarding a flight to Charleston when Usher called him."

"Did you get the password?"

"No! He said my father's instructions were adamant that any information about that account had to be given to Emily or me personally. He wouldn't budge on that. He said his flight arrives at 8:15."

Decker looked at his watch. "Okay, it's 6:45 now. Here's what's going to happen. I'll have Osborne and two other officers get you to the airport to meet that lawyer. I'll be at the warehouse with our SWAT Team. We'll monitor the situation and wait for your call once you've met that lawyer. Detective Glass will station a group of officers outside the Blue Dolphin. I'll let him know if and when to move on Coldwell."

"What do I do when I get the new password?" Joe asked.

"That depends on how much time we have left before the kidnappers call you back. You said the lawyer gets in here at 8:15. By the time he deplanes and gets to the exit, it'll be 8:30. That gives us about an hour until you get the call at 9:30. If it works out like that, you and the officers will have plenty of time to get to the warehouse, and we'll wait for the call together."

"Why don't you just go into the warehouse and get Emily now?" Joe asked.

"First of all, we're not sure she's there," Decker answered. "We wait. When you get the password, you'll give it to them, and we'll hope they release her." Despite what he'd just said, Decker understood kidnapping statistics. The harsh truth is that more than 80% of kidnapped victims never survive their ordeal. In this case, he believed the chances of them letting Emily go were slim to none.

"If I give them the password, how am I going to get Emily back? If she's not at the warehouse, then I'm going to have to meet them somewhere else. They're going to expect me to be driving my truck."

Decker was embarrassed he'd completely missed the fact that Joe didn't have his truck at the station, but he attempted to cover himself. "Of course, the officers will take you to get your truck and then make sure you get out to the airport."

"What about the $10 million?" Joe asked. "Once they have the password, they'll be able to move the money."

"Let the DEA and FBI chase it down," Decker said. "Three people were murdered on my watch, and I want the sons-of-bitches that did it! Now let's get moving. No screw-ups."

Decker left the conference room just as Officers Kelly and Pryor entered. Osborne made the introductions. It was decided that the three officers and Joe and Alex would take one squad car to pick up Joe's truck. Officer Kelly would then accompany Joe and Alex in the truck, with Officers Pryor and Osborn continuing to the airport in the squad car.

Joe, Alex, and Officer Kelly pulled into the airport at 7:30 and parked directly behind Pryor and Osborne at the main entrance. An airport officer approached, and Pryor said a few words to him. The officer nodded and walked away.

As he entered the terminal, Joe checked the digital displays. Delta flight 1744 out of Atlanta was now scheduled to arrive ten minutes early at 8:05.

Airport security required all arriving passengers to leave the two main concourses through a single terminal exit. There was a large area just outside the security gate where people could wait for arriving passengers. There were couches and chairs arranged throughout the waiting area, and Joe, Alex, and the officers took one of the seating areas next to the security exit. Pryor called Decker, advising him that the lawyer's flight should be landing in about a half-hour.

"So, what's this Bellamy guy look like?" Officer Kelly asked Joe.

Joe kicked himself for not asking Usher or Bellamy himself. "No clue." But Joe had to smile when he said, "Three cops and the two of us—I think he'll find us."

Thirty-five minutes later, Joe was eyeing the exiting passengers when a tall man in a dark blue suit walked into the waiting area. He was scanning the room. Joe stood and approached with his hand extended. "Mr. Bellamy, I'm Joe Nash."

"Uh, okay, great," the man said before sliding around Joe to join a woman who'd been waiting for him.

Joe's anxiety grew. *What if Bellamy was somehow held up or he missed him?* Just then, a man approached where Joe and the officers were gathered. He was dressed in jeans, a black open-collared shirt, and a tan corduroy sport coat. Joe thought he looked like a college kid.

"Excuse me, gentlemen, would one of you be Mr. Joseph Nash?"

"That would be me," Joe said. "You must be Mr. Bellamy."

"Yes, sir. If you could follow me, please."

Officers Pryor and Kelly stood and started toward Bellamy. "Hold on," Pryor said. "Mr. Nash needs to stay with us."

"I understand perfectly, officer. We won't be leaving the area. I have some confidential information for Mr. Nash and need to discuss that information in private."

Pryor looked at Kelly, who nodded his agreement. "All right, just stay where we can see you."

Bellamy led Joe about 50 feet away to where their conversation could not be overheard.

"First of all," Bellamy began, "I need to ask you if you are here of your own free will. Can you assure the bank that you will use the password for you and your sister's benefit and that no one has coerced you to use it in any other manner?"

"I told Mr. Usher my sister's been kidnapped. Hell yes, I'm going to use it for our benefit!"

"I realize that, Mr. Nash. Please understand that your father had placed several caveats on us when he established this account. I am simply required to ask these questions."

"All right. Anything else? I need that password."

Bellamy removed an envelope from his briefcase. He opened it and handed a small sheet to Joe. It read: *cyyoung1061911*.

A smile spread across Joe's face. "Cy Young pitched his last game on October 6, 1911."

"That's interesting, but you'll need to memorize the password." Bellamy extended his hand to retrieve the paper.

"No problem," Joe replied and returned the paper to Bellamy, who ripped it into small pieces and put them in his pocket.

Bellamy handed Joe his business card. "I hope this helps you get Emily back safe and sound. You can call me if you have any questions."

Joe thanked him and headed for the exit—waving for the rest of the group to follow.

CHAPTER 19

MICHAEL FERRARI AND Theo Jackson were seated in the Blue Dolphin office when Coldwell arrived at his restaurant that evening. He was unaware the men would be there. He was taken aback but quickly gathered himself.

"Gentlemen, good to see you," as though he'd been expecting them. "Can I get you something to drink?"

Both men remained seated and silent.

The awkward silence was broken when Coldwell said, "Are you sure I can't get you something?"

"As a matter of fact, you can, Eli," Ferrari said. "You can get us the money you owe us. You've had your forty-eight hours—actually, a little more than that."

"You'll have your money in an hour," Coldwell said, his voice uneasy. "Marvin and a few of his men have Nash's daughter. As soon as we get the new password for the Belize account, I can transfer the money back to our account in the

Cayman Islands. Then I'll give Marvin the order to eliminate the girl and her brother."

"Well, if you don't mind, I think Theo and I will just hang around until that happens."

CHAPTER 20

JOE, ALEX, AND Officer Pryor left the airport and headed to Coldwell's warehouse to meet Detective Decker and Chito Walker's SWAT team. They had a little less than sixty minutes before the kidnappers were to make their final call.

Kelly and Pryor had orders to rendezvous with Decker and the SWAT Team at an abandoned dock off McMillan Avenue. The staging area was about a half-mile from Coldwell's Hipp Street warehouse. Chito Walker had already reconnoitered the scene, finding two cars and a white cargo van in the rear.

When they arrived, Joe and Alex were taken to an area behind an armored vehicle and three Humvees. Decker saw Joe and waved him over.

"Nash, what's the password?"

"C-y-y-o-u-n-g-1-0-6-1-9-1-1," Joe called it out slowly, and Decker jotted it down.

"All right, we've got about twenty minutes until we get the call. The SWAT Team will deploy in ten minutes. Whatever you do, don't give them the password until they agree to return your sister."

"I won't, but what are we going to do if she's not inside that warehouse?"

Decker pointed to Joe's Ranger. "Chito's people are putting a GPS tracker on your truck now. You're right; they might tell you to go somewhere else. If that happens, we'll be able to follow your movements. From now on, I want you with me. Osborne has the Octopus set up."

Decker led Joe and Alex to where Osborne had the system set up in the squad car's trunk. Three members from the SWAT team were stationed around the trunk, too. They were dressed in full tactical gear, including level IIIa body armor, protective helmets and eyewear, assault webbing for holding magazines, knee pads, gloves, and rappelling harnesses. Each carried an AR-15 assault rifle or a 12 gauge tactical pump shotgun and a semi-automatic sidearm. Their presence was daunting. A few minutes later, Decker got confirmation that SWAT was in place at the warehouse.

"Okay, Nash, it's almost 9:30. Remember, they get nothing until we get your sister. You need to know Chito has the authority to move on the warehouse if he feels it necessary. Be firm with the caller but not aggressive. Try to keep your emotions in check. I'll be listening, so if there's …"

Decker's instructions were interrupted by Joe's cell. Decker and Osborne slipped on their headphones.

Joe answered and said, "I want to talk to my sister."

A half-laugh could be heard, and the modified voice answered, "Mr. Nash, you are to get into your Ford Ranger by yourself and drive to the Harley-Davidson Store on Dorchester. I repeat, *by yourself.* How long will it take to get there?"

"About twenty minutes," Joe said.

"Good. If we see anyone with you, I will begin by cutting off one of Emily's ears. Understood?"

"Yes. Just don't hurt my sister."

The line went dead.

CHAPTER 21

JOE JOGGED TO his truck with Decker, Alex, and the three SWAT officers right behind him. He jumped in and was about to close the door when Decker stopped him.

"Two SWAT officers are going with you. They'll stay hidden in the bed of your truck and do nothing unless the situation requires intervention."

"You heard what they'll do if anyone's with me! They'll cut off her ear!"

Decker nodded to the SWAT officers, and two of the three climbed into the truck bed and covered themselves with a brown tarp.

"Calm down," Decker said. "We've been involved in multiple kidnappings. These men will improve our chances of getting your sister back alive. Trust me on this. They know what they're doing. Now go! SWAT Officer Williams will come with us. He'll be tracking your movements. Good luck!"

Joe was pissed but knew he didn't have time to do anything about it. He slammed the door and took off—burning rubber as he left.

Decker and SWAT Officer Williams took off running for an unmarked Crown Vic. Decker slid into the driver's seat, Williams next to him. Decker was on the phone waiting to advise Chito when Alex pulled open the rear passenger door and jumped in.

Decker covered his phone and yelled, "Get the hell out of my car!"

"I'm not going anywhere!" Alex shouted. He then lowered his voice. "I promise I'll stay out of the way. He's my friend. He wants me with him. I swear you won't even know I'm here."

"Not this time!" Decker shouted.

Officer Williams turned toward Decker. "Do you want me to remove him, sir?"

"Wait," Decker said and stared at Alex. "Leave the car now, or I swear I'll have you arrested."

Knowing he had little choice, Alex reluctantly got out of the car.

Decker started the Crown Vic and pulled onto McMillan and followed Joe's truck.

~~~~

Joe headed down McMillan and turned left onto Meeting Street, which ran into Dorchester. Once on Dorchester, it was
~~~~

only a few miles to the Harley-Davidson store. A few minutes later, he pulled into the store's empty parking lot.

His phone rang less than thirty seconds later.

"Excellent so far, Mr. Nash. I have someone watching you as we speak. Do you see the black Nissan Sentra in the parking lot?"

Joe saw the Nissan at the far end of the lot. "Yes, I see it."

"You are to exit your truck and get into the Nissan. Keys are in the ignition. Leave your cell phone in your truck. There is another phone in the Nissan. You will receive a call on that phone when you get in the Nissan."

Joe stepped out of his truck and saw one of the SWAT officers raise the tarp just enough to see. Without looking at him, Nash whispered, "Stay in the goddamn truck. They're watching me! Don't fucking move until well after I'm gone. I'm getting in a black Nissan Sentra. I can't see the license plate. Stay where you are!"

The SWAT officers remained hidden while Joe got into the Sentra. As soon as he shut the door, a phone on the passenger's seat rang. He answered it.

"Congratulations, Mr. Nash. So far, so good. Your sister still has both ears. Here's what you're going to do next. Take 526 South and get off at exit 11A. Then take Ashley River Road North. We'll stay on the line with you. And know that if this call is disconnected for any reason, your sister will become hard of hearing. Understood?"

"Yes. Where am I going?"

"I'll tell you when I need to. Relax and enjoy the ride, Mr. Nash."

~~~~

Decker was headed to the Harley-Davidson store, and Officer Williams was monitoring the GPS when he noticed the tracker showed that Nash's truck had reached the store and stopped in the parking lot. Williams had the cell numbers of his fellow two SWAT officers in Joe's truck and texted one of them.

"Stanton, this is Williams. What's happening?"

Officer Stanton reported that he and his partner were still in the truck and that Nash was now in a black Nissan Sentra. He texted back, "Target leaving the parking lot now."

Williams passed on the information to Decker that Nash had changed vehicles and was leaving the parking lot.

"Son-of-a-bitch!" Decker blurted, slamming his hand onto the dashboard. "Why the hell did they let him leave!"

Officer Williams wasn't about to let the detective question his fellow officers' decision to remain in the truck. "There is no question the kidnappers have eyes there, sir. If they had exited the truck, the operation would have been jeopardized, and Nash or our hostage may have been harmed! They made a tactical decision!"

By now, they were approaching the Harley-Davidson store. Officer Williams first spotted the Nissan. "Sir, the Nissan just pulled out of the lot!"
~~~~

Decker saw the car but held back. Joe was now on Paramount Street, heading toward the 526 South ramp. Not knowing whether Joe was by himself in the Nissan, Decker stayed well behind while maintaining visual contact.

It was well after ten, and the freeway traffic was light. Williams had his binoculars trained on the Nissan but couldn't determine if anyone were in the car with Nash. Then, suddenly, the Nissan's overhead light turned on, and the interior was visible.

"Smart move up there, Nash," Williams said. "He looks to be the only one in the vehicle."

Decker sped up to get closer. And when Nash turned off 526 about six miles later, he followed him onto Ashley River Road.

"I'm on Ashely River now," Joe told the kidnappers. "Now what?"

"Good boy, Mr. Nash. Continue for four miles until you see a cemetery on your left. Live Oak Memorial Gardens. Enter the cemetery and take the first right. Go a short distance, and you'll see another turn-off to the right. Take that and continue until it runs into the edge of a wooded area. Stop there, exit the car, and wait. Is that clear?"

"Yes. Then what?"

"Relax, Mr. Nash. Just do what I told you, and Emily will remain fit as a fiddle. Just don't hang up."

~~~~
~~~~

Decker followed Joe when he turned off 526 onto Ashley River Road. He continued down Ashley River until he saw the Nissan make a left turn. Decker slowed when Joe pulled into the cemetery. He eased the Crown Vic forward in time to see the Nissan make a right inside the grounds.

"What now?" Decker asked Williams.

"Continue slowly," Williams directed. "We should be able to see if Nash continues straight or turns off that road."

Decker pulled up and saw Joe turn right again and slowly move down a narrow road. The Nissan continued until it reached the edge of the woods and stopped. Joe got out and stood by the car.

"Move ahead until you see the edge of that tree line," Williams ordered. "Go a little bit beyond and pull off the road."

Decker drove forward to past the edge of the woods and pulled onto the berm. "What now?"

Williams brought up Google Earth on his field-modified iPad. The world spun until it offered a clear vision of the cemetery. It was surrounded by a densely wooded area.

Williams and Decker exited the Crown Vic and moved to the edge of the woods. From that vantage point, they could see the Nissan parked about 75 yards down the tree line. "Follow me. We'll use the trees as cover," Williams said and removed his AR-15. Decker followed Glock in hand. "Let's go! Move it!"

It was clear SWAT Officer Williams was now running the operation.

Williams turned and gestured for Decker to stay down and behind him. They crossed the street and entered the woods about twenty feet from the tree line. Williams looked through the woods—eyes scanning until he froze and dropped to a knee. Decker followed suit.

"Nash is by the Nissan. I can see three men just inside the tree line. I'm not positive, but it looks like the girl is with them. We wait and watch. They'll do nothing until they get the password and confirm it's legitimate."

Williams sent a text message to Chito Walker, informing him he had located Nash and the kidnappers and was monitoring the situation. He added his GPS coordinates to the text and requested backup.

A few moments later, one of the kidnappers stepped forward and said something to Joe, who walked just inside the tree line. He was dwarfed by the black man who looked to be a half-foot taller and at least seventy-five pounds heavier. He was holding a phone to his ear. Joe handed a paper to the big man, who looked to be reading its contents to someone on the other end of the line.

Williams maintained visual contact with Nash and the black man for a few minutes before turning back to Decker. "Here's what I want you to do. Move behind the three men and take a position at ten o'clock relative to the tree line. Stay there. Be careful." Williams had served tours in both Iraq and Afghanistan and knew the crazy things men do when they're faced with someone trying to kill them. "You'll know when to move on the kidnappers."

"Yeah, how?"

Williams held up his AR-15 he'd been carrying. "Let's just say I'll use this to interrupt their concentration. It's been about five minutes since they got the password. I expect as soon as the funds are transferred, they intend to kill Nash and his sister."

CHAPTER 22

COLDWELL'S MACBOOK PRO displayed a SCOTIA-BANK account number and a dropdown menu for the password.

Coldwell typed in the new password: C-y-y-o-u-n-g-1-0-6-1-9-1-1. He hesitated to depress the enter key, afraid the funds would not be there. He took a deep breath and hit enter; he was in—$10,245,756. He turned to look at Ferrari and Jackson.

"What did I tell you? Take a look at this!"

Ferrari smiled.

Coldwell then entered the necessary commands to transfer the entire amount to his original WESTPAC account in the Cayman Islands.

The three men watched as $2,049,151 appeared in his WESTPAC account, leaving a balance of $8,196,605 with SCOTIABANK.

Ferrari's face turned sour. "Where's the rest of our money?"

Coldwell was confused. Only 20% of the total funds were transferred into the WESTPAC account.

"Eli, I said where the hell is the rest of the money?"

"I don't know. Hang on, and I'll find out."

Coldwell searched and found the phone number for the SCOTIABANK in Belize City. It was after 10:30, but he knew these banks had officers on call 24/7. He put his phone on speaker and placed the call. He was put on a short hold before he was connected with a banker. After verifying the account information, the banker explained that there was a covenant attached to it that limited withdrawals and transfers to 20% of the account balance. He said he could transfer another 20% one hour after the original transfer.

He further explained that withdrawals or transfers could be made after each additional hour until the balance fell below $1,000,000. At that point, restrictions were lifted. Coldwell disconnected the call.

"All right," Ferrari said. "We got it. It's just going to take a little while." He turned and nodded at Theo.

Theo returned the nod and said, "Eli, it's time to remove Nash and his sister."

"I agree," Coldwell said and made the call.

"Yeah?" Simms answered.

"Eliminate both of them. Understood?"

"Yes, sir."

~~~~

"Okay, Mr. Nash. You did a bang-up job. Your sister is fine, but she's a bit confused. We gave her something to calm her nerves." Simms reached back, took Emily's arm, and pushed her forward.

Joe lunged and caught her just before she fell.

"Everything worked out just fine, Mr. Nash—that is, except for one little problem." He waved his two men forward. "And the problem is you both know who I am. We just can't have that—now can we?"

Simms' men both carried Sig Sauer P365 9mm pistols fitted with Obsidian 45 noise suppressors. "It's been nice knowing both of you—especially Emily. She's a real looker."

The kidnappers flanking Simms started to raise their guns. Joe and Emily were in Williams' line of sight. Rather than chance it, he opened up with his AR-15, spraying all 30 bullets into the trees directly above the kidnappers. Terrified, all three men hit the ground as branches and leaves rained down. Joe pulled Emily close and stumbled backward, also falling. His adrenaline spiked as Williams discarded his assault rifle, removed his Glock, and advanced.

Hearing the gunfire, Decker's blood pressure and adrenaline also amped-up as he scrambled forward on his elbows and knees, stopping behind the base of a tree where he could see what had just unfolded. Decker was now in a position to get off a shot at the man on the far left. But before he could fire, the man spun toward him and fired several rounds, one winging
~~~~

Decker in his left shoulder, but he felt no pain—the adrenaline doing its job. He dove right, rolled over, and returned fire, hitting the man in the arm and chest.

A second kidnapper caught sight of Williams as he approached the clearing and opened fire. Williams heard the "thud, thud" of sub-sonic rounds. Both rounds hit a tree to his left—sending wood shards in front of his face. He heard the hiss of a third bullet as it passed close. He dropped to one knee and had his Glock raised, but before he could pull the trigger, a fourth bullet slammed into his Kevlar® chest protector. He dropped his gun as the force knocked him back. The kidnapper's next two rounds hit the ground short of Williams, spraying dirt and leaves.

All six of his rounds spent, the kidnapper removed a knife from his ankle sheath and charge Williams. A second later, the man was on top of Williams, swinging his knife. Williams caught the man's wrist with both hands and twisted the knife back toward his attacker. The knife plunged into the man's chest right below the collarbone. The man screamed as Williams rolled on top of him. A vicious blow to the side of the man's head rendered him unconscious. Williams retrieved his Glock and staggered forward.

By now, Decker had his gun holstered and was helping Joe and Emily get up. Williams, clutching his chest, began surveying the grounds for the big man until he saw that Simms had taken off in the melee and was almost to the cemetery entrance. Williams knelt and raised his Glock, holding it with both hands. He exhaled, held his breath, and fired off four rounds—two catching Simms in the thigh and back. He went down, tried to get back up, but fell again.

Williams then turned back to the two kidnappers, both of whom were on the ground. "Stay down, or you will be shot!" he shouted.

As if on cue, three police cars entered the cemetery and headed across the lawn toward Williams and Decker stood. One of the cars skidded to a stop next to Simms, who was again trying to stand. One officer jumped out with his gun drawn and shouted, "Freeze! On the ground now!"

Simms fell forward and remained motionless as the officer cuffed him.

Less than a minute later, more police cars appeared, and the night exploded in a sea of blue and red light.

CHAPTER 23

WILLIAMS WAS ON the phone advising Chito Walker that Nash and his sister were safe, and the kidnappers had been subdued. Decker was taking in the scene when he turned to Williams and smiled. "You certainly interrupted their concentration."

"You did good, sir," Williams said and noticed blood seeping through Decker's shirt and dripping onto the ground. "Now you need to get that arm taken care of."

As his adrenaline waned, the severity of Decker's shoulder wound became more apparent. Officers escorted him to a squad car, and they headed to MUSC. On the way, Decker called Glass, letting him know that Nash and his sister are safe, and three kidnappers had been wounded and were in custody.

"Justin, I need you to move on Coldwell."

"You got it."

Joe held his sister close and whispered, "Hey, little sister, you're going to be all right." Her eyes were dilated, and she made no response, still under the influence of whatever drug Simms had given her.

Officer Williams put his hand on Joe's shoulder. "Are you okay, Mr. Nash?"

"I'm fine, but we need to find someone to take care of my sister."

"Is she able to tell us if there was anyone else involved in her kidnapping?" asked Williams.

"I doubt it," Joe answered, "she's not responding at all. She's been drugged."

"Okay, then, follow me, sir."

EMS had not yet arrived, so Officer Williams led Joe and Emily to where two officers stood and told them to take the two to MUSC.

The officers helped Emily into the squad car, and Joe joined her in the back seat. He shut the door and leaned out the window. "Officer Williams, sir. I just wanted to thank you for everything you did tonight. You saved our lives."

Williams nodded his acceptance, slapped the car's roof, and it left the cemetery for downtown.

~~~~

It was after eleven when Glass ordered his officers to enter the Blue Dolphin. The restaurant was empty except for a few men still at the bar. They watched as six officers in full Kevlar®
~~~~

vests and headgear carrying ArmaLite M-15 carbines moved through the dining room to Coldwell's office.

Glass nodded to an officer, who opened the door and stepped aside. Glass and the remaining officers followed. "Hello, Mr. Coldwell." He turned to Ferrari and Jackson. "Well, what in the world are you two doing here so late at night?"

Despite being caught by surprise, Coldwell managed to close the browser on his computer while Glass addressed Ferrari and Jackson.

"I'm not sure you're aware, Mr. Coldwell, but a few of your men have been arrested. Actually, they were involved in some gunfire tonight, and all three were wounded. I'm going to have to take you down to the station and see if you can help sort this out." Glass nodded to an officer to pat the three of them down. He removed a .38 Special from Ferrari and a Berretta M9 from Jackson. Coldwell carried no weapons.

Glass told Ferrari and Jackson they were free to go.

"What about our guns?" Jackson asked.

"Do you have your permit?"

"I have one, but not with me."

"How about you, Mr. Ferrari?"

"It's in my car."

"I'm sorry about that, gentlemen, but you know you need to keep those permits on your person. I'm afraid I'm going to have to take those guns with me. You're more than welcome to bring those permits by and pick up your firearms at the Lockwood station tomorrow morning."

"You have no right to do that," Ferrari protested.

"Well, I just did." Glass responded. "Deal with it. Now you can leave on your own accord, or my officers will be more than happy to escort you out—your choice."

They were leaving when Theo caught sight of Coldwell. His stone-cold glare left no room for words. Glass told two officers to take Coldwell to the station and hold him there.

One of the remaining officers pointed to Coldwell's desk and computers. "Sir, should we see what's in his desk? Maybe take a look at that computer?"

"No can do!" Glass replied in no uncertain terms. "We don't have a search warrant. You should know better, officer."

"Of course, sir. Sorry, sir."

"We're finished here. Let's head back to the station."

Back in the car, Glass called Decker to report what he'd accomplished at the Blue Dolphin. He also wanted to learn more about what transpired with Nash, Emily, and the kidnappers. His call rang several times before it was finally answered by a woman. "Mr. Decker is unavailable. Please call back later."

"This is Detective Glass. I'm his partner."

"I'm sorry, sir. We're just bringing him into the emergency room. Can I give him a message?"

"The emergency room. What emergency room?"

"This is MUSC, sir. I'm sorry, but I'm going to have to cut this short."

"What happened to him? Just tell me!"

"Gunshot to the left shoulder. He'll be okay, sir. Don't worry. Now, I really have to go." The line went dead.

Glass told the officer driving to forget about the station and take him directly to MUSC. The officer turned on his flashing lights and siren and headed downtown at high speed. Glass called the officers taking Coldwell to the station and told them to sit on him until he got there.

Chapter 24

IT WAS A long and harrowing night for all involved.

Williams remained at the cemetery, preserving the crime scene until two detectives from Lockwood arrived to take over the investigation.

Officers dropped Joe and Emily at MUSC's Emergency Room, and after a forty-five-minute wait, the attending physician examined Emily and had her blood drawn and analyzed. The results would be back in twelve hours, but he said she should most likely be just fine after a good night's rest.

It was after one Thursday morning by the time the doctors dealt with Decker's gunshot wound. Glass remained at the hospital with his partner and drove him home after he was released. Decker said he'd be at Lockwood at nine Thursday morning to give Glass a break. Glass returned to the station and began interrogating Coldwell.

Everyone finally did get some sleep that night, except for Glass and Coldwell, who'd been deposited in a conference room the night before. Glass told the officers that if Coldwell complained too much, they should let him know a jail cell and a few roommates were waiting for him at County Detention Center.

Decker was exhausted when they arrived at the station. The sedation and pain meds he'd been given the night before had long since worn off. His arm was in a sling and hurt like the devil, but he wouldn't take additional meds. He wanted pure focus while dealing with Coldwell and the investigation.

The two detectives were in their cubby having coffee when Captain Stone and Steve Gagyi joined them.

"Well, you two look like shit," Stone said. "How's that arm, Max?"

"Hurts like hell, but you know what they say—*protect and serve*, right, Captain?"

Stone smiled. "What's the plan with Coldwell?"

"Justin spent a couple hours on him earlier this morning. No luck so far, and his lawyer is already here, waiting out in the lobby."

"Why does that not surprise me?" Stone said. "How about the three that were arrested out at the cemetery last night?"

"All three received gunshot wounds," Glass replied. "They're in the hospital—one of them is in the ICU."

"Justin has been up all night," Decker said. "I'll head over to the hospital and see what I can get from them."

"I figure Coldwell's lawyer will start demanding we let him go," Glass said. "We don't have enough to arrest him yet, but I figure we can hold him a few more hours. If we get nothing by then, we'll have to cut him loose."

"Justin's right," Decker said. "Let's face it, the only thing we have right now that comes close to connecting Coldwell to Mr. Nash's murder is the fact that Coldwell was Nash's biggest client. That doesn't really prove anything. Obviously, Rice and the lawyer were close to Nash, but that also doesn't prove Coldwell was involved in their murder. Unless we can get something from those three in the hospital, we've got zero connections between Coldwell and the murders of Nash, Rice, and Gallo."

Stone looked at Gagyi. "Steve, tell them about those accounts."

"Yes, sir. Please bear with me. This may get a bit confusing. We have access to the accounts in both the Cayman Islands and Belize. But Coldwell does not know we have the account number and password to his Cayman Islands account. I checked both accounts last night after the shootout and found that $2,049,151 appeared in Coldwell's Cayman Island's Westpac account, and a balance of $8,196,605 remained with Scotiabank in Belize. Obviously, Coldwell must have transferred the $2 million from Scotiabank to Westpac."

"Okay," Decker said, "I'm with you so far."

"Good," Gagyi continued. "So I checked again early this morning, and the $2,049,151 was still in the Westpac account; however, the Scotiabank account showed a zero balance."

"Wait a minute! What happened to the $8 million in the Belize account?" Decker asked.

Everyone was quiet for a moment before Stone finally said, "We have absolutely no idea."

~~~~

Stone and Gagyi left for the observation room to watch the interrogation, and Decker and Glass entered the conference room to grapple with Coldwell.

"I've had enough of this crap," Coldwell said. "When the hell can I get out of here?" He looked like shit, the dark circles under his eyes extending almost to his blotched cheeks.

"We trust you enjoyed your stay last night," Decker said. "How'd you like our accommodations?"

"Listen to me, Decker. I was patient the last time you brought me in here. I can't believe your partner and his gang of wannabe Rambos broke into my restaurant last night and embarrassed me in front of my friends!"

"Sorry you feel that way, but you're here to answer a few questions. The first is: What happened to all that money you had in the Cayman Islands?"

"I already told your partner I have no idea what you're talking about. Where is my lawyer?"

"Any messages for your friend Marvin Simms?" Decker asked. "I understand he's in the hospital fighting for his life. We sure hope he makes it. I bet he'll have a lot to say when he recovers."
~~~~

This was the first time Coldwell heard anything about Simms being seriously injured.

There was a knock on the door, and a short man in a tan suit entered. "Eli, don't say another word. Gentlemen, my name is Shelton Beckerman, and I represent Mr. Coldwell. I understand he was arrested last night. May I see the arrest warrant?"

"Actually, counselor," Glass said, "your client has not been arrested. You see, there was a kidnapping last night, and a few of Mr. Coldwell's associates were involved. And during that kidnapping, those associates shot a police officer." He pointed to Decker's sling. "We were hoping Mr. Coldwell could help us in our investigation."

"I suggest you either charge my client or let him go immediately," Beckerman demanded. "My client was at his restaurant last night and had nothing to do with what you are talking about."

"Mr. Beckerman, your client is only a person of interest," Decker calmly responded. "We plan to talk with him for another few hours. We should be finished this afternoon. You're free to return then to pick up your client."

Beckerman stood. He knew the detectives were within their rights to detain Coldwell before either charging him or letting him go. After shooting the detectives a virulent stare, Beckerman said, "We'll just see about that. I'll be talking with the DA about this."

He pulled Coldwell aside and whispered, "Don't tell them anything. I'll be back to get you."

Beckerman stormed from the conference room, slamming the door as he left.

Glass gave Decker a look, and the pair got up and left without a word.

Coldwell was left wondering what happened at the cemetery. He'd ordered Simms to eliminate Nash and his sister but had no idea that Simms or his men had been involved in a firefight with the police or that Simms was seriously injured.

Decker and Glass entered the observation room. Glass, a touch of sarcasm in his voice, said, "Well, that was informative."

"Captain," Decker began, "there's probably no way we can hold Coldwell much longer. We'll put a tail on him when we let him go. We may not have anything solid yet, but we know damn well he's behind these murders."

Stone agreed and told Decker he also planned to have his officers tail Ferrari and Jackson. "I don't have any doubt those two are also part of this thing. They're still out there, so I've ordered an officer stationed outside of the house where Joe Nash and Emily Nash are staying. Steve checked on Coldwell's men in the hospital this morning. Tell them what you learned, Steve."

"Marvin Simms is in intensive care," Gagyi began. "A bullet caught him in the leg and blew open his femoral artery. He lost a ton of blood and went into hypovolemic shock before EMS could get the bleeding stopped. He also took one in the back. That bullet hit his lung, tore his pericardium, and nicked his heart. His lung collapsed, and he had extensive bleeding in the chest. They've got him in the ICU at MUSC. The last thing I heard, he was on a ventilator and in surgery."

"Jesus, Gagyi, you sound like a doctor," Decker said.

Gagyi grinned. "Well, I was Pre-med before the computer bug bit me. A friend of mine is a resident at the hospital. I called him this morning."

"Simms is Coldwell's main man," Stone said. "No doubt he orchestrated Emily's kidnapping."

"What about the other two guys?" Glass asked.

"Their injuries weren't as serious as Simms', plus those two were just hired hands. We've got them in custody in the hospital, but they've got no direct connection to Coldwell."

Glass left for the Bunkhouse, a room where detectives and officers could catch some sleep while working a case. Decker arranged for undercover officers to watch Coldwell, and he left for MUSC to be there if Marvin Simms regained consciousness.

~~~~

Joe and Emily spent the balance of the night with Alex at his house. Joe put Emily—who was still under the influence—in the second bedroom, and he slept on the couch. Alex took the day off and had breakfast ready when Joe rolled off the couch and shuffled into the kitchen.

"How do eggs, sausage, toast, and a big cup of coffee sound?" Alex asked.
~~~~

"Sounds great!" Joe replied. "I had this weird dream last night. I was running around a cemetery, and people were shooting at me."

They'd just sat down to eat when Emily's phone rang. Joe answered it and listened for a moment.

"Who was that?" Alex asked.

"Her doctor. He got the results of the toxicology screen. Apparently, the guys holding Emily were injecting her with butorphanol, a pain drug like morphine."

"No wonder she was so messed up," Alex added.

"Exactly, but the doc said the body metabolizes it quickly, and she shouldn't feel any effects when she wakes up."

"Speak of the devil," Alex said as Emily walked into the kitchen.

"Good morning, beautiful," Joe said.

"I don't feel so beautiful. Do we have coffee?"

"Comin' right up," Alex said and poured her a cup.

She slumped into a seat at the table. "Who wants to tell me what happened last night? It's all pretty fuzzy."

"I bet it is," Joe said and told her about the butorphanol. He went on to tell her everything he knew about the kidnapping.

"God, I got to call Cindy. Is she okay?"

"I talked to her," Joe offered. "She was pretty shaken up, but she's all right now, so I wouldn't worry."

"I still need to call her. I remember we were both asleep when those men came in the middle of the night. I couldn't do anything. They gave me something that made me feel really strange. I'm sorry, Joe. They told me they had you and would kill you if I didn't tell them about Dad's account in Belize. After I told them I didn't know the account number or password, they gave me a shot of something, and I don't remember anything after that. God, I didn't know how close I came to being killed."

"Well, your safe and sound now," Joe said.

Alex got the okay from his landlord to have a locksmith come out and change the locks and install deadbolts on the exterior doors to be on the safe side. Joe, Emily, and Alex spent the afternoon and evening recovering from their ordeal and relaxing at the house.

Chapter 25

COLDWELL AND HIS lawyer were out of Lockwood shortly after three Friday afternoon. Beckerman drove to Hampton Park, where they sat in his car and talked.

"I should sue those bastards," Coldwell seethed.

"You can't do that, Eli. They had a right to hold you—although it was a shitty thing to do. Now, listen to me. I understand your man, Marvin Simms, is in serious condition. The question is: Do you have any exposure to what happened at that cemetery?"

"I heard he was hurt bad," Coldwell answered—dodging Beckerman's question. "But even if he survives, he won't talk."

"That may be true, but let's just assume he does survive, and he does talk. That would put you in a difficult situation. Am I correct?"

"Perhaps," Coldwell said.

"Well then, let's hope he doesn't make it," Beckerman said.

~~~~

Decker had been in the ICU waiting room for several hours. Simms remained in critical condition but was now breathing on his own. Decker was growing restless but wanted to be there the minute Simms regained consciousness.

Glass showed up at the hospital at 4:30 that afternoon with sandwiches. He had slept for a few hours and felt better.

"Is Coldwell at his place?" Decker asked.

"Yeah. The lawyer just dropped him off. Our officers are camped out on Broad Street watching his house. Anything new on Simms?"

"A little. He's had surgery and is still in critical condition, but he's been taken off the ventilator. So, that's good news."

"He's still not out of the woods, is he?" Glass asked the obvious.

"No, but he's a whole lot better than he was."

They'd just started in on their sandwiches when they heard a commotion from down the hall. They both put their sandwiches aside and moved toward the tumult—hoping Simms had regained consciousness.

A nurse had just run through the door to the ICU. Glass caught the door before it closed. They saw frenzied activity surrounding one of the patients. A doctor, who was frantically
~~~~

giving instructions to the nurses, saw them and yelled for them to get out.

"Christ, Justin, that's Simms they're working on!"

The doctor and several nurses moved in an orchestrated flurry around his bed. Decker's eyes went straight to the heart monitor behind Simms. All of a sudden, **its** rhythmic beep turned into a loud and continuous beeeeeeeeeeeeee! He all flatlining!

"We've got a code blue!" the doctor yelled. "Get me the crash cart!"

A nurse had already started cardiopulmonary resuscitation when the crash cart was wheeled next to Simms' bed. The doctor grabbed the defibrillator pads, his eyes riveted on the flatlined heart monitor when he shouted, "Clear!"

He initiated the controlled electric "countershock" to the heart. The line on the monitor remained flat—the high-pitched death-tone unbroken.

"Clear," he shouted again and repeated the process three more times until the frenzied action subsided. Apart from the monitor, the ICU went deathly quiet. The doctor looked at the clock on the wall. "Noted. Time of death; 4:50 p.m., Friday, September 10th."

"Son-of-a-bitch," Decker said, a bit too loud.

The doctor swung an exhausted gaze his way. "You really shouldn't be here."

The detectives quickly retreated to the waiting room. Decker picked up his sandwich and threw it in the trash. "I just lost my appetite."

Nothing more needed to be said. They knew Marvin Simms was their only direct connection to Coldwell. And without that connection, they had no substantive evidence linking him to the murder of Frank Nash, Michelle Rice, and Anthony Gallo.

~~~~

Decker and Glass returned to Lockwood and went directly to Captain Stone's office.

"We're screwed, Captain," Decker admitted. "Simms just died. He was our only direct link to Coldwell—and Ferrari and Jackson for that matter."

"How about Nash and his sister? Do you have them covered?" Stone asked.

"Yes, sir. Nash's sister is staying at his friend's house with her brother. We've got officers stationed outside. The officers following Coldwell reported that he was dropped off at his house on Broad Street about an hour ago."

Stone's cell rang. "Hang on a second." He answered it and listened for less than a minute before speaking into the phone. "Okay, hook up with them. Send someone behind the house to cover the rear exit. Right. See if you can get someone close enough to hear what's going on in there. Be careful and keep me posted." Stone hung up. "That was the crew I had following Ferrari. He just showed up at Coldwell's with Jackson and another man. Coldwell let them in the back door. Our crews are on it."
~~~~

"This has to be about those offshore accounts and what happened at the cemetery," Glass said. "And also, I doubt they know Simms is dead."

"You said another man was with Ferrari and Jackson," Decker said. "Did your officers identify him?"

Stone frowned. "I'm afraid they did."

"Who is it, Captain?" Glass asked.

"Bobby Watts. He works for Jackson. He's like Coldwell's Marvin Simms—only more skilled with a knife and gun."

Chapter 26

WATTS HAD DRIVEN a dark brown Chevy Impala and parked it in the rear of Coldwell's house. The Chevy would be later chopped at a salvage company Jackson owned—removing any chance it could be found. Watts, exiting the car along with Ferrari and Jackson, went directly to the trunk and removed a large black suitcase.

Coldwell let Ferrari and Jackson in the back door but hesitated a second when he saw Watts was wearing gloves and carrying the suitcase.

Ferrari closed the door behind Jackson and Watts.

"What happened after the cops took you last night, Eli?" he asked. "What did you tell the detective?"

"I told him nothing!"

"That's good because Marvin Simms and his two boys put on a real shitshow last night," Jackson added. "I hear he got his ass shot up real good. I don't give a fuck about him. But I do care about getting the rest of that money. How's that going, Eli?"

Coldwell turned beet red. "There was a problem."

"A problem?" Ferrari questioned. "What problem?"

"That detective kept me at the police station all last night, and I never got a chance to continue transferring the money out of the Belize account. I was just about to start moving the rest of it when I ran into a problem."

"Didn't you hear me the first time?" Ferrari raised his voice. "What problem?"

"The $2 million I transferred last night is still in our Westpac account, but for some reason, I can't find the funds in the Scotiabank account in Belize. I'm sure it's a glitch in their system. I was going to call the bank and clear it up."

"Well, Eli," Jackson said, "I suggest you clear it up right now."

Coldwell led the three men back into his office and used his desk phone to dial the number for the SCOTIABANK in Belize City.

"Put the call on speaker, Eli," Ferrari instructed. "We want to hear this."

The call was answered, and after a brief hold, a banker came on the line. "May I have the account number and passcode you are referencing, Mr. Coldwell?"

Coldwell passed on the information.

"Yes, sir. I see there are no funds in that account," the banker responded quietly.

"That's impossible!" Coldwell clamored. "I never transferred any money from that account after last night. Where did the money go?"

"I'm sorry, sir. All I can say is the funds must have been removed from that account. There are currently no funds available, sir. Is there anything else I can help you with?"

"Hell, yes! I want to know who took the money!"

"Again, sir, I'm afraid …" The line went dead.

Coldwell looked at the phone and saw Jackson had disconnected the call.

"Where's the money?" he asked.

Droplets of perspiration were forming above Coldwell's upper lip. "I don't know. It doesn't make any sense. You saw me create a new password for the Belize account last night. Nobody else knows what it is except me."

"Exactly," Jackson said, "Now, I'll ask you one more time. Where's the money?"

"I told you. I don't know."

Jackson stepped back and nodded to Watts. "Bobby, see if you can help Eli remember where he sent the money."

Watts removed a .22 LR semi-automatic handgun. The weapon was compact and whisper-quiet, always his choice for close-up wetwork.

Before Coldwell could react, he heard a thud, and his left foot exploded in pain. He grabbed his foot and moaned through clenched teeth, "Son-of-a-bitch."

"Does that refresh your memory?" Jackson calmly asked.

"Damn it, Theo! I told you I don't know what happened."

Another thud and his right foot was on fire.

Jackson leaned in close. "Bobby just ran out of feet, Eli. Do you want him to start on your hands?"

"Please, you got to believe me. I don't know where the money went. I promise!"

"Hold it, Bobby," Jackson said. "Eli might need those hands when he remembers where he sent that $8 million. Be creative."

Watts put away his .22 and removed a switchblade. He grabbed Coldwell's hair, yanked him forward, and ran the blade across the back of his head. Blood poured from the wound and ran down his neck.

"Did that help your memory, Eli?"

"Please," was all Coldwell could muster.

"I take it that's a no," Jackson said.

Watts placed the blade under Coldwell's chin and lifted his head with it. A small trickle of blood escaped the knifepoint.

"I really don't think he knows, Theo," Ferrari said.

"Okay, Eli. Just give us the password for the Westpac account with the $2 million."

Coldwell mumbled, "8-Y-O-G-I-B-E-R-R-A-1-9-6-5."

"Got that, Michael?" Jackson asked. Ferrari nodded. "Now, Eli, give us the new password for the Belize account."

"0-7-0-6-5-2-b-l-u-e."

"Did you get that, Michael?"

"Got it."

"Go ahead, Bobby," Jackson said.

Watts walked behind Coldwell, placed the knifepoint against the back of his neck just below his hairline, and thrust it up. Coldwell immediately went slack and fell to the floor. Watts removed a cloth from his pocket and wiped the blade clean.

Ferrari pointed to the security camera mounted above the office door. "Bobby, disconnect that. There's also one just outside the front and back doors. You'll need to take them both."

As soon as Watts had the office camera stuffed in his suitcase, Jackson pointed at the computer on Coldwell's desk. "Grab that and his cell, and let's get the hell out of here."

Shortly after Ferrari, Jackson, and Watts had entered Coldwell's house, one of Stone's officers had crept up to the house and heard the gunshots. He waved his partner forward and used hand gestures to communicate the situation. They took up positions behind bushes on either side of Coldwell's back door. Another officer activated his shoulder radio and called in a 10-31—crime in progress—and a 10-32—firearms present. "Officers need backup, 112 Broad Street."

They silently entered the back door, guns drawn, and hearing voices, moved toward Coldwell's office.

Watts was about to disconnect the computer when four plainclothes police officers burst through the office door; their Glocks trained on the men and yelled, "Freeze! Don't move, or you will be shot!"

All three were taken entirely by surprise. "Move away from the computer! All of you slowly raise your hands above your head!" They did as they were told. "Keep your hands raised and drop to your knees. Lay forward, flat on the ground! Do it now!"

Ferrari and Jackson dropped to their knees. Watts hesitated until he looked at the four barrels leveled at his chest.

"Hands behind your back!" Two officers kept their firearms pointed at the men while the other two secured the suitcase and cuffed them. They remained flat on the ground—heads down and hands cuffed—as officers removed weapons from all three.

The wail of sirens cut through the fading light of a Charleston night.

~~~~

Decker, Glass, and Stone arrived at Coldwell's house in less than ten minutes. The officers were cordoning off the area with yellow crime scene tape. A few neighbors had started to gather.

Stone looked at Decker and Glass and pointed at the house. "Go ahead, detectives. It's your investigation."

Decker and Glass took over the scene—issuing directives and stationing the officers. Decker ordered Ferrari, Jackson, and Watts to be separated and taken to Lockwood. Once the exterior crime scene was secured, they entered the house. An officer stood outside Coldwell's office—his face ghost white.

"In there," was all he said.

"Are you okay?" Decker asked.

"Yes, sir."
~~~~

Decker told him to go outside and get some air. The last thing he needed was someone getting sick at his crime scene.

Decker and Glass entered the office and recoiled at the horror—Coldwell sprawled on the floor. Blood pooled around his feet—head and neck wounds visible.

Decker was focused on Coldwell's body when Glass said, "Max, look at that computer." The screen still showed the name and logo of the Scotiabank in Belize City. Glass moved forward, careful not to step in the blood. He pointed at the bottom of the computer screen. "There it is. Just like Gagyi said. All the money in Belize is gone!"

"There's no doubt Coldwell was killed because of that," Decker added.

Forensics arrived and asked to get started.

"Have at it," Decker said. "We'll be outside if you need us."

Once outside, Decker nodded at Glass. "You stay here and make sure everything runs smoothly," he said. "I'll see you back at the station. I want to get started on our suspects."

Chapter 27

JOE LOOKED OUT of the living room window Saturday morning and noticed the car and the two police officers were gone. "Hey, Alex. It looks like Starsky & Hutch took off."

Alex joined him at the window. "Listen, Joe, now that this is behind you, I wanted to talk to you about your plans."

"My plans?"

"Come on, Joe. What are you going to do about baseball?"

"I don't know," Joe replied and gave a half-hearted laugh. "The last few months, my curve didn't curve enough, and my fastball wasn't fast enough."

"I remember how I felt when I blew out my Achilles. I know I would have been drafted—maybe not in a high round, but at least I would have had a shot at playing professional ball. It about killed me, but I moved on. The question is: What are you going to do?"

With all the chaos and drama over the last week, thoughts about his future had been on hold. He was finished for this season—he knew that much. But he also knew that Baltimore was aware of his MRI results and would want a decision from him sooner than later. He'd known several pitchers who'd had Tommy John surgery, and research showed that over 80% of the surgeries were successful. He also realized how long recovery would be and that rehab would be brutal.

Before Joe could reply, Alex said, "You're the best damn pitcher I ever caught, but I also know there are no guarantees in baseball. Whatever you decide, you'll end up okay."

"Thanks, Alex." Joe was quiet for a moment before continuing. "All right, I haven't told anyone this. I'm leaning toward law school, and about a month or so ago, I went ahead and applied. I got accepted to the University of South Carolina, but I still haven't made up my mind. I've got some time, but management is going to want to know about the surgery pretty soon."

"I guess it's good to keep your options open," Alex said. "I think you can make it, but don't forget about James Newberry. He said he'd be more than happy to help if you decide on law."

"That's good to know," Joe said. "At least I've got some time to figure things out. I'll tell you one thing, being back here in Charleston made me realize how much I missed my sister and the city."

"Yeah, I know. It's a pretty cool place to live, and Emily is special. I've got to run. Shannon's parents are in town for the weekend, and I'm going to be tied up the rest of today and tomorrow."

Joe laughed. "Don't mess that thing up, boy. I think Shannon's a pretty awesome lady."

"I couldn't agree more," Alex said. "We've been together for almost a year, and it keeps getting better. What are you up to today?"

"Emily wants to go back to her apartment. I'll drop her off later this morning and probably chill for the rest of the afternoon. Em and I are going out to dinner later." Joe had just finished talking when his phone rang. He answered and listened for a moment. "That works. We'll see you in about an hour."

"Who was that?"

"Detective Glass He wants Emily and me to stop by the station this morning. He said they've got some more information."

"Interesting," Alex said.

~~~~

Emily and Joe got to Lockwood and were ushered into a conference room where Decker, Glass, and Gagyi were waiting.

"Good morning, folks," Decker said. "We wanted to bring you up to speed with some developments in our investigation."

"Good developments or bad developments?" Joe asked.

"Good, we think," Decker said. "Justin, why don't you go ahead?"
~~~~

"Sure," Glass said. "As you know, the kidnappers were taken into custody at the cemetery. Two of them sustained treatable gunshot injuries, but the man who organized the kidnapping eventually died. His name was Marvin Simms, and he worked for Eli Coldwell."

"What happened to Coldwell?" Joe asked.

"We'll get to that in a minute, but first, Officer Gagyi will tell you about the offshore accounts in Belize and the Grand Caymans."

Steve explained that after Coldwell received the new SCOTIABANK password the night of the cemetery shootout, he was only able to transfer 20% of the account to his WESTPAC account in the Caymans. At that time, Glass and his men detained Coldwell—stopping him from making any additional transfers.

Decker picked it up from there. "Michael Ferrari, Theo Jackson, and another man named Bobby Wats were with Coldwell the following day when he logged into the SCOTIABANK account only to find that all the money had disappeared. We believe Watts murdered Coldwell because of this. All three men have been arrested."

"Where did the money go?" Emily asked.

"We have no idea," Decker answered. "We're turning everything over to the Justice Department. They'll be working on attempting to recover the money in the Cayman Islands' account and finding the missing $8 million from the Scotiabank account."

"So all this means we're safe now, right?" Emily asked.

"Yes," Decker said. "You can go ahead and live your lives knowing there's no longer a threat."

~~~~

Joe dropped Emily off at her apartment and returned to Alex's place. With nothing to do, he was left to ponder Alex's questions. He thought back to the last time he had to make an important decision about his baseball future when he had to decide whether to sign a professional contract or stay in college. He'd gone to Coach Lee then—why not now?

Joe made the short drive across Charleston Harbor to the Patriots Point field. Their regular season wouldn't start until mid-February, but the new Cougar recruits began to work out in September. It had been almost ten years since Joe stepped onto this field and started his college career. He remembered it as if it were yesterday. Joe hung behind the right field fence, watching outfielders shag flyballs and pitchers throw on the sidelines.

He was watching for about fifteen minutes when he heard, "Well, I'll be damned! That young fella sure looks like Joe Nash!"

Joe turned and saw Coach Lee walking up the first baseline—a huge smile plastered across his face. Joe waved at Lee, walked around the fence, and jogged toward him. Lee grabbed his hand and said, "If it isn't my favorite left-handed
~~~~

pitcher. Joe, it's good to see you. What brings you to Charleston?"

Joe explained that his father had died and was in town for the funeral. He left it at that.

"I'm sorry, Joe. I didn't know."

"Thanks, coach. It's good to see you." Joe pointed to the pitchers. "How do they look this year?"

"We've got a good group. They'll need a lot of work, but the potential is there. How's your career going? I heard you're still with the Orioles."

"Right," Joe said. "Triple-A in Virginia. Actually, if you've got a minute, I wanted to talk about that."

"Sure." Coach Lee knew Joe well enough to know something was wrong. "What's going on?"

"My elbow," Joe admitted.

Lee knew immediately it was the UCL. "How bad is it?"

"The doctor said it's a moderate tear." He was quiet a moment before saying, "Coach, I can't throw the way I used to. They put me on IR."

Coach Lee put his hand on Joe's shoulder. "Surgery?"

"Yeah, Tommy John. Sounds like it's my only real option. I'm just not sure what to do."

"Let's take a walk," Lee said. "You know I was drafted out of high school by the Dodgers. I was good but not good enough to make it past Double-A ball, and it took me four years to finally accept it. I have an idea of what you're going through. I also know I can't tell you what to do. But what I can tell you is that you've got the tools, and with that surgery, I have no doubt you'd have a shot. But that last jump to the major league is always the toughest. You'll figure it out. Just know that there is life after baseball."

"I know it's my decision, coach. I'm just not sure I can wait another two years."

Lee patted Joe on his back. "Come on, I want you to talk to my recruits. They all know about Joe Nash. They'd get a kick out of meeting you."

Joe spent most of the afternoon with Coach Lee and his players. He enjoyed working with the young guys and passing on some things he'd learned on his baseball journey. He left late that afternoon with a promise he'd come back and see his coach and the young recruits again.

Joe was back at the house just a few minutes before Emily called. "Hey, big brother, how about that dinner you promised?"

"You got it, Sis. It's Saturday, so we better get going if we're going to get in anywhere. Give me a few minutes to clean up, and I'll be right over. How about Mellow Mushroom?"

"Sounds good," Emily said.

Joe changed and was washing his face when his phone rang out in the living room. He quickly dried his face and answered it.

"Good afternoon, Mr. Nash. This is James Bellamy."

Joe was surprised to hear from Bellamy and stammered a bit before saying, "Mr. Bellamy, it's nice to hear from you."

"I hope I'm not interrupting you."

"No, sir. Not at all."

"Good," Bellamy began. "I was hoping we could get together. I have some items to discuss with you and your sister."

"Wait, you're in Charleston?"

"Yes, downtown at the Francis Marion Hotel. There's a Starbucks right off the lobby here. We could meet there this evening—if that works for you."

"Sure." Joe checked his watch. "How about six?"

"Perfect," Bellamy said. "I look forward to seeing you again."

Joe hung up and stood there, processing what he'd just heard. *Why the hell would Bellamy want to see us?* He called Emily with the change in plans asking her to meet him at the Starbucks across from Marion Square.

Emily was waiting when he arrived at Starbucks, and Joe told her the latest with Bellamy. She was just as surprised as he was.

"What could he possibly want?" Emily asked.

"It's got to have something to do with Dad and the bank."

"Weird."

Joe checked his watch and saw they were about ten minutes early for their meeting with Bellamy. As usual, Starbucks was crowded, but Emily spotted a table.

"You want a coffee, Em?"

"If I get one, does that mean you're not going to buy me dinner?"

Joe smiled. "No, dinner is included."

"Okay, I'll have a latte."

Joe picked up two lattes and returned to the table just as Bellamy stepped inside. He made his way over, shook Joe's hand, and turned to Emily. "Miss Nash, it's a pleasure to finally meet you—and under better circumstances, I might add."

"Nice to meet you," she said. "We were a little surprised to hear from you."

"I imagine you were. It's such a beautiful evening. Wouldn't it be nice to take a walk in Marion Square?" It was more of a statement than a question. They crossed King Street, entered the park, and found a bench away from the main pathways. "Let's sit for a while," Bellamy offered.

"How long are you in town?" Joe asked.

"I'm afraid only for a day," Bellamy answered and quickly turned the conversation to his reason for being there. "As you can imagine, I'm here regarding the account your father set up with our bank in Belize. The stipulations he placed on the account were extraordinary, to say the least. I can't go into too many specifics. However, I can assure you that it was your father's intention that the funds would eventually be transferred to both of you."

"The police told us that money disappeared," Joe said. "And they have no idea where it went. As you can imagine, we've been wondering about that."

"I don't doubt it," Bellamy said. "Your father was aware that there were certain parties who would take extraordinary measures to divert those funds. One of his provisions required that after the first withdrawal was made, the remaining money was to be automatically transferred to another account with our bank." Bellamy removed an envelope from his jacket and handed it to Joe. "Let's just say that this was your father's final gift."

Joe opened the envelope, removed a sheet of paper, and showed it to Emily. It read:

NOSCBZBSXXX9485730081

thebambino714

$8,196,605

Love, Dad

Bellamy stood. "I'm sure you will use it wisely." He again gave both Joe and Emily his business card. "I'll be your contact should you have any questions or require assistance with your account. We should talk in the next few weeks. I can explain how the account works and the different ways you can use the funds, and our fee structure. It's been a pleasure meeting you both. I'm going to go for a walk and take in some of your beautiful city before I have to go back home. Again, it's been a pleasure."

Bellamy stood, nodded, and walked away—leaving Emily and Joe on the park bench, fully dumbfounded.

"Joe, did we just get $8 million?"

"I think so," Joe responded, his eyes glued to the paper he held in front of him. "To be more specific—eight million, one hundred thousand, six hundred and five dollars."

Emily looked at it. "What's 'thebambino714 mean.'"

That brought a smile to Joe's face. "It's Babe Ruth's nickname. He hit 714 home runs."

"This is part of the $10 million Dad took from Coldwell," Emily said. "Joe, that's dirty money. You heard what Decker said—prostitution, gambling, drugs, stuff like that."

"You're right, Em, but we can use it to do good—like giving money to causes we believe in. But whatever we do with it, it has to be anonymous."

A smile appeared on Emily's face. "Like a million dollars toward breast cancer research? I think Mom would like that."

"Yeah," Joe said, "that's what I mean, and we can use Bellamy to set it up."

"Joe," Emily said, the smile frozen on her face, "I can't believe Dad did this."

"I think he finally came to realize all the selfish things he'd done in his life. He wanted to make amends, and this was the way he did it."

"Whatever you do," Emily said, "don't lose that paper."

"I won't." He pointed to the sheet and smiled. "I think this is enough to cover dinner tonight." He put his arm around Emily. "Come on, little sister, dinner is on Dad tonight."

EPILOGUE

Oriole Park at Camden Yards

IT WAS LATE April, the sky clear and the air cool as a light breeze wandered out of the east carrying the scent of the sea. The bright lights illuminated the field of green, and the iconic B&O Warehouse towered high above the right field stands. The cheers of forty thousand fans filled the confines of Camden Yards as the Orioles took the field.

Joe Nash stepped from the dugout and jogged to the mound. It had been two long and arduous years since his surgery—years filled with thousands of hours of sweat and pain as he slowly strengthened his left arm. He was confident it was now stronger and more flexible than it had ever been.

He finished his warmups and waved his glove over his head, signaling his catcher to throw the ball to second. The shortstop caught it and started the ball around the horn, ending with third baseman Ryan Bannon. Bannon trotted toward Joe, stopping about fifteen feet from the mound.

He flipped the ball to him and said, "Hey, Nash, welcome to the Show."

Joe walked to the back of the mound, faced centerfield, and took a deep breath. He looked up, pointed to the heavens, and sent a message to his mother. He turned around and looked just above the Orioles' dugout to where Coach Lee was standing next to Alex and his wife, Shannon—all of them waving. Next to Shannon was his sister, Emily, holding up a sign that read, *"Good Luck, Big Brother!"* She blew a kiss and gave a thumbs up.

As Joe placed his right foot on the pitching rubber, the roar of the crowd disappeared, and his world turned silent. His attention was focused solely on the catcher as he went through the series of signs. Joe leaned in and nodded—fastball.

Joe Nash had a smile on his face as he went into his windup, reached back, and let it fly.

A WILD RIDE

Chapter 1

A HINT OF a smile appeared on Michael Coppola's face as he disconnected his cell phone and stared at the gray-haired man sitting across from him. "The rest of your money has been deposited like you instructed. Are you sure this was a clean job? No loose ends, as they say?"

The gray-haired man returned Coppola's stare for an uncomfortable moment before saying, "I'm not in a business that tolerates loose ends, Mr. Coppola. The individual you desired eliminated has been eliminated. It was clean. No loose ends, as they say."

Michael Coppola was a bull of a man. He'd lifted weights when he was young, but he'd had lost interest over the years, and it was clear that good food and drink had gotten the upper hand. His hair combed straight back; his pants belted a bit too high above his waist.

The gray-haired man had met Coppola only once before and took an immediate dislike of him. This was unusual. Having worked in his particular profession for over twenty years, he'd always divorced himself from any emotional reaction to his clients or why they required his services. Emotion could be deadly in his line of work. The gray-haired man knew Coppola's operation played a relatively insignificant part within the Organization, and as a rule, he would not have even entertained a contract from him. However, one of the upper-level bosses also expressed an interest in removing the target and made a recommendation he accept the contract—recommendation being the operative word.

The gray-haired man stood and removed a small plastic baggie from his pocket. There was a key inside the baggie, and he placed it on the desk in front of Coppola.

"As agreed, you are to dispose of the vehicle."

"That will be taken care of," Coppola replied.

"Good, then we are done here."

The man stood and turned to leave but stopped when Coppola asked, "Where's the body?"

The comment confirmed the man's opinion of Coppola. "That is not your concern. It has been dealt with. I suggest you leave it at that."

The gray-haired man left the backroom of Callaghan's Bar and Grill, a room that Michael Coppola considered his office. His "office" looked more like a storage room with brown cardboard liquor boxes stacked against one wall. Metal shelving resembling the kind found in warehouses lined the opposing wall and held various restaurant and bar supplies. Coppola had several framed photos of himself taken during his trips to Italy and a few gaudy Italian travel posters hanging on the wall behind his desk. His associates took great pleasure in reminding him that he was Italian and worked out of the back of an Irish bar.

Coppola remained seated for the next few minutes contemplating his next moves. He'd never been involved in murder for hire before, but his bosses had sanctioned the hit. Plus, he had no regrets about taking out a contract on Cornell Jackson. Coppola considered Jackson to be a two-bit punk-ass pissant—but this pissant and his boys had been picking away at his prostitution and drug business for the past six months. His operation was relatively small, and he'd always paid his agreed-upon percentage to the Organization and kept his business within the boundaries assigned to him. *Shit*, he thought, *I should have done it sooner.*

He stood and walked outside of his office into the back of the bar lit only by a fluorescent light hanging over a well-worn pool table. He scanned the bar until he saw Jimmy Sanborn, one of his collectors. He called out to him, and Sanborn made his way back into the office. "Shut the door and sit down," Coppola said. "Who you got working tonight?"

"Gino and Vic are handling the girls," Sanborn answered.

"Who else you got?"

"Buddy's at home with the family, but the new kid, Eddie Russo, is here. What'd you need done?"

Coppola tossed the baggie with the key in it to Sanborn. "There's a brown Honda Civic parked behind the bar. Tell Russo to take it out to Park's Auto Salvage on Hall Road in Goose Creek and make sure Gino gets it. I told him he's getting a car tonight. He knows what to do with it."

"How's Eddie going to get back?" Sanborn asked.

"Anyone else out there?" Coppola asked.

"Just Eddie. You want I should call Gino or Vic to come in?"

"No," Coppola said. "I need them working the whores. They'll steal us blind if nobody's watching them. I'll have one of Gino's guys at the salvage shop give him a ride."

"All right," Sanborn said, "I'll take care of it."

"One more thing, Jimmy," Coppola said. "Tell Eddie to keep his fucking mouth shut about this."

Sanborn returned to the bar and gave Eddie Russo the baggie with the key in it and told him a brown Honda was parked behind the bar. "Do you know where Gino Vitale's salvage shop is?"

"Yeah," Jimmy answered. "Out in Goose Creek, right?"

"Right. On Hall Road. Gino's expecting a car to be delivered to him later today. Mr. Coppola wants you to drive it out there and give it to him. He'll get rid of it. You do this and then you forget you did it. Understand?"

"Sure. No problem, Jimmy," Russo said. "Do I get a couple of bucks for this?"

Sanborn put both hands on Russo's shoulders and leaned in close. "I know you're new around here, Eddie, so here's some advice. If Mr. Coppola asks you to do something, and you ask for money, you're asking for trouble. Capisce?"

"Okay, okay. I got it. Does Gino know what kind of car he's getting?"

"I don't think so, but that's none of your business," Sanborn said. "Just drive the car out there and make sure Gino gets it."

"I ain't got my car here. How am I going to get home?"

"Gino will have someone drive you back to your place. Remember to keep your mouth shut about this."

Eddie finished his beer and walked around the back of the bar to where the Honda was parked. He thought the shit-brown color sucked, but other than a couple dings and scratches, it looked in pretty good shape. He slid in the driver's seat, removed the key from the baggie, and started the car. The odometer read 61,375 miles. The interior wasn't that clean, but other than that seemed to be in decent shape. He started going through the glove compartment and pulled out the owner's manual—surprised to find the car's title and registration. The title listed the Honda as a 2012 LX Coupe.

He drove out of the bar and headed down Rivers Avenue towards Goose Creek. Jimmy knew the car would be chopped for its parts and then crushed at Gino's shop. *What a fricking waste*, he thought. His car was a 2008 Chevy Malibu with almost 120,000 miles on her. Both rear shocks were gone, and it was on its last leg. Plus, it had been in a few fender benders, and its lower side panels were rusting through. He'd be lucky to get $1,500 for it.

"What the hell," he said out loud and turned into a McDonald's on Rivers. He bought two cheeseburgers and a Coke and pulled into a parking spot. *All right, think this thing through*, he thought.

Eddie figured he might be able to give Gino the Malibu and keep the Honda. He remembered Jimmy said he didn't think Gino knew what kind of car he was getting from Mr. Coppola. Plus, he had a few burner phones and two phony driver's licenses. There'd be no problem fudging the back of the title. He removed his cell phone, searched Kelly Blue Book, and found out he should get around seven thousand dollars for the Honda. If he sold the sucker, he could buy a half-way decent car and put a couple grand in his pocket. It was too good to pass up. When he got back to his apartment, he rummaged through his stuff until he found the title for his car. He drove the Malibu out to the salvage shop and delivered the Malibu to Gino.

The following day, he created a bogus Facebook page and put the Honda on Facebook Marketplace. He was surprised when he got a message thirty minutes later from a guy asking about the Honda.

Chapter 2

RYAN WOODS WAS looking forward to a well-deserved week-long break from his job as a Junior Engineer at the Boeing facility in North Charleston, South Carolina. He'd just tossed his briefcase onto the passenger's seat of his Silverado when his cell rang. He glanced at his phone and saw it was his good friend Vince Kelly. Vince had been home for about a month after finishing six years as a field officer in the Marine Corps Special Operations Command—spending the majority of his deployment in Afghanistan and Yemen. As part of the Special OPS team, Vince was often called upon to use his unconventional combat skills in counter-terrorism and special reconnaissance operations. Much of what he did during his military service was classified and involved cross-border interventions that sometimes required deadly enemy interactions. Vince rarely, if ever, spoke about what he did during his career in the Marine Corps.

"Well. It's finally done," Vince said.

"Are you serious? How'd it go?"

"Katy and I pretty much just sat there and let the lawyers hassle over the last few stupid-ass things before we signed the papers. It only took about forty-five minutes—all very nice and civil. Katy even gave me a hug and a kiss on the cheek before she left the law office."

"Are you okay with everything?" Ryan asked. "I mean with how the settlement worked out?"

Vince laughed. "Ryan, we were only married three years—no kids, no mortgage, no vacation home on the beach. We split the money in the joint savings account—which wasn't all that much. She'll get everything in the apartment, and I'll have to pay half the rent until the lease is up. Oh, and she also got the car. That was about it."

"I'm sorry it didn't work out," Ryan said. "I really liked Katy."

"Yeah, I know. Who knows why we didn't make it? Being overseas sure as hell didn't help. I think we just expected too much of each other. Anyway, we'll stay friends, and that's a lot more than most people can say." Jason laughed again. "I guess we didn't stay together long enough to hate each other."

"So, what are you going to do now?"

"I've got to find a damn job," Vince answered.

"No, I mean like right now," Ryan said.

"Well, I'm out of the apartment, so I need to find a place to live," Vince answered. "Plus, I've got to get a car."

"You can crash at my place until you find an apartment."

"Thanks, I really appreciate that," Vince said.

"No problem. Listen, I'm leaving work. Where are you now?"

"I'm still at the Halstead Law Firm by the Citadel Mall."

"Stay put. I'll google it and be there in about twenty minutes," Ryan said. "I say we pick up a case of beer and head back to my place. We can get you settled and talk about getting you some wheels."

"Sounds good," Vince laughed. "I'll pay for the beer; you can provide the electricity."

Ryan Woods and Vince Kelly grew up together in Mt. Pleasant, South Carolina. Their friendship was solidified in the sixth grade when Ryan was walking home from school and ran into three middle school boys. They started to hassle Ryan and had knocked him around pretty good before Vince showed up. Vince was not only sizable for his age but had grown up in a family that valued toughness. Vince took a pretty hefty beating himself but doled out enough damage to the middle schoolers to save Ryan from an even worst drubbing.

Both boys were excellent athletes, with Ryan excelling in basketball and baseball while Vince earned his stripes on the football field. Vince was awarded second-team All-State honors as a defensive end on Wando High School's football team in his senior year. Not to be outdone, Ryan led his Warriors' baseball team to the conference championship and was named the All-Conference shortstop. Ryan had always been a good student and attended Clemson University, where he earned his engineering degree. Vince had a slew of college football scholarship offers but decided to enlist in the Marines right out of high school. His father and grandfather had been marines, and there was never any doubt Vince would follow in their footsteps.

With Ryan away at school and Vince deployed overseas, the boys didn't see much of each other. They did, however, stay in contact whenever possible. Time had done nothing to diminish their friendship.

Ryan pulled up in front of the lawyer's office, and Vince tossed his large two-strap, camouflaged Marine Duffle Bag in the back seat of the truck and got in. They stopped at the grocery store and picked up the case of beer, chips, and two steaks. Ryan was putting the beer and food in his back seat when he noticed Vince's Duffle Bag. "Is that everything you got?"

"No. I rented one of those self-storage units out on Ashley River Road." He gestured toward his Duffle Bag. "That'll get me by until I find a place."

"Well, like I said, you can stay at my apartment as long as you need to. Now, let's see if we can put a dent in that case of beer."

~~~~

Ryan rolled out of bed the next morning at eight o'clock and was surprised to see Ryan sitting at the kitchen table wearing a U.S Marine T-shirt drenched in sweat.

"Jesus, Vince, don't tell me you've been out running already."
~~~~

"Yep. I try to do about five miles every morning. Old habits are tough to break. Plus, if I remember correctly, we drank a hell of a lot of beer last night, and I wanted to sweat it out."

"You're right about the beer," Ryan said, "but I prefer to deal with my hangovers with aspirin, scrambled eggs, hash browns, and a few cups of black coffee."

Ryan made breakfast while Vince showered and dressed. They ate and spent the next hour looking through Craigslist and Facebook Marketplace for apartments. Vince found a few possibilities they planned on visiting that afternoon.

"Now, let's see if we can find you a car," Ryan said.

Vince was checking Facebook Marketplace when he said, "Ryan, take a look at this one." He was looking at a photo of a 2012 Honda Civic listed for $7,000. "It's only got about 60,000 miles. It's more than I wanted to spend, but it might be worth taking a look at. What do you think?"

"Definitely," Ryan said. "How much can you spend?"

"I got about $15,000 in the bank, but I figure I'll need about $3,000 for the apartment's rent and security deposit. I've also got to get a bed and some furniture. Plus, I don't know how long it'll take to find a job, and I don't want to strap myself. I was thinking a max of about $6,000 for the car."

"Why don't you just send the guy a message and get some more information on the Honda. If it sounds good, we can take a look at it."

Vince responded to the message on Marketplace, and after going back and forth with a few more messages, he got the person's information and agreed to meet him at the Centre Point Apartments in North Charleston that morning at 10:30.

~~~~

One of Eddie Russo's buddies lived at the Centre Point Apartments and gone to Atlanta for the weekend. He was waiting next to the Honda in the apartment's parking lot when Ryan and Vince arrived. Eddie knew they would be in a black Silverado and waved at the truck when he saw it pulling in.

"There's he is," Vince said, and Ryan parked the Silverado a few spaces from the Honda. "Look's okay from here. Let's check it out."

They got out of the truck and saw what looked like a kid standing next to the Civic. Vince introduced himself and Ryan and after asking a few questions about the car, asked, "Do you mind if we take it for a spin?"

"No problem," Eddie replied. "The keys are in it. I'll just wait here."

Vince had just turned onto Glenn McConnell Parkway when Ryan commented that the car hadn't been washed, and while the interior looked okay, it could use a good cleaning. Despite this, it drove smoothly with no obvious mechanical problems. Vince pulled into the Lowe's parking lot, popped the hood, and did a quick inspection of the engine. It looked good.

They made it back to Centre Point Apartments ten minutes later. "The car drove okay," Vince said to the kid. "If I can ask, why are you selling it?"
~~~~

Eddie figured he'd be asked that and had come up with a story. "I just moved here from Columbia, and the job I got includes a car. So, I don't need the Honda anymore."

"I'll be perfectly honest with you," Vince began. "I hadn't planned on spending that much. Would you be willing to work with me on the price?"

"Depends on what you're willing to offer."

"I just got out of the marines, and all I can handle is $6,000. If that works for you, I can get you a certified check from the bank this morning."

"Hey, man," Eddie responded, "I checked Kelly Blue Book, and it said I should get seven thousand bucks."

"Maybe so, but that's all I can afford."

Eddie let out his breath and did not immediately respond. He was disappointed with the offer, but what the hell? If he got the $6,000, he could still pocket a grand after he got himself a decent car. "I'll tell you what," he said, "if you give me the $6,000 in cash now, I'll do it."

Vince almost laughed at the guy. "I don't have that kind of money on me. I said I can go to my bank and get you a certified check."

Eddie was using a fake name and knew he couldn't take a check of any kind. "I want cash," he said. "You can get cash from the bank."

Ryan pulled Vince away from Eddie and whispered, "I doubt you're going to find anything as good at that car for that price. I'd tell him you want to see the title, and if everything seems on the up and up, I think you should get the cash and buy the car."

Vince returned to where Eddie was standing. "Okay, but I'd like to see the title if you don't mind," Vince said.

"No problem," he said. "It's in my apartment. Wait here, and I'll be right back." Eddie had put the title under the mat in front of his friend's apartment. One of the fake licenses listed an address in Columbia, South Carolina, and he'd used that on the back of the title. He waited a few minutes before returning to the parking lot. "Here you go," he said and gave Vince the title.

He looked and it and showed it to Ryan. "Looks okay to me," Ryan said.

"All right," Vince said. "My bank is open until noon today. I'll get the cash and be back in about forty-five minutes. What's your apartment number?"

"Just call me when you're on your way back," Eddie quickly answered. "I'll meet you out here."

Vince looked at Ryan, and he nodded. "All right," Vince said, "we'll be back in less than an hour."

It took about forty-five minutes to get to his bank and withdraw the cash. On the way back, Ryan told Vince to get a leather portfolio in his truck's back seat. "There's some paper and a pen in there. Write out a quick bill of sale for the Honda. Leave a blank for the VIN number and a place for both your signatures."

"What address should I use for the bill of sale and title?" Vince asked. "Remember Katy's still living at our old apartment, and I won't be there anymore."

"I know, but I'd go ahead and use that address anyway—your driver's license and all your other identification list that address. You can change it after you move into the new apartment and go to the DMV. You'll need a new driver's license anyway."

Ryan called the number the guy had given Vince and told him they be back in a few minutes. Eddie Russo, who used the name, James Alexander, met them Vince and Ryan when they returned. The title and a simple bill of sale were filled out and signed. Vince gave Eddie the six-grand, got the keys to the Honda, and followed Ryan out of the lot and back to his apartment.

~~~~

Ryan and Vince spent most of the afternoon checking out several apartment complexes—finally deciding on a one-bedroom in West Ashley at a place called Grand Oaks. It was another three weeks before the unit would be available for him to move in.

They got back to Ryan's apartment around four o'clock. "Let's give your new wheels a bath," Ryan suggested. "I was surprised the guy didn't even clean it up. There's an area in the back of the apartments with water outlets that we can use to
~~~~

wash the car. I'll get a bucket, some rags, and cleaning supplies and meet you back there."

After they finished with the outside of the Honda, Vince said, "I'll get started on the inside, and you can use the handheld vac and work on the trunk."

"Works for me," Ryan answered, popped the trunk, and found clumps of dried mud and a large dark stain in the center of the carpet. "Jesus Christ, what a frickin' mess!" He used his hands to remove the larger clumps and then tried to suck up what was left of the dirt with the vac. There was no way he would get all of the stains out—even after scrubbing it with soap and water. He finally gave up and began helping Vince finish up with the interior.

Vince was vacuuming the carpet under the front seat when he noticed a small piece of paper that had fallen between the front seat and the center console. He tried to get to it, but his hands were too large. "Hey, Ryan, come here a minute." He pointed under the front seat. "See that paper? Can you reach it?"

Ryan bent down and slid his hand between the console and metal frame at the bottom of the front seat. He could barely get to it, but after a few tries, he finally able to pull it out. He'd just crumpled it up when Vince asked him what was on it.

Ryan smoothed it out. "It's an address." He passed it to Vince.

The piece of paper was small, and Vince had to look close to read it. "It says, Cornell Jackson, *2131 Stall Road, Tri-County*

Apts." Vince figured he would pitch it when he finished with the car and stuffed it in his pocket.

Vince got out of the car and stretched his back. "Hell, Ryan, she cleans up pretty good, doesn't she?"

"Yeah, it looks like a different car."

The guys were putting away the rags and cleaning supplies when Vince mentioned he would need to go to the DMV and get a new title, registration, and plates.

"Right," Ryan agreed, "but there's no rush. You've got forty-five days to do it. It's almost six o'clock. I say we go back to the apartment, grab a couple beers, and get something to eat."

"I thought you'd never ask," Vince replied with a smile.

Chapter 3

NOAH MARTIN'S 280-ACRE farm had been in the family for five generations. It was located about 40 miles from Charleston off Highway 17 South in Colleton County. Noah raised a small herd of beef cattle; however, his main cash crop was feed corn.

Like most days, Noah was up this Sunday morning at 4:30 a.m. He planned on doing some wild hog hunting before taking his wife, Elizabeth, to church. For years, these wild hogs—often called feral pigs—had done significant damage to his corn crops, as well as spread disease and polluted the streams and ponds on his land. The hogs ate his corn and damaged his fields by their rooting, trampling, and wallowing behaviors. A few of his neighbor farmers' livestock had been hit with an outbreak of Bovine tuberculosis caused by these wild hogs.

Like many local farmers, Noah had purchased the necessary equipment at the Army Surplus Store to hunt the hogs. He'd had been tracking a particular hog for about twenty minutes through a relatively dense wooded area when he heard the familiar sound of hog grunts and snorts coming from about thirty yards up ahead. Noah swung the Winchester Model 70 .30-06 off his shoulder and moved forward as quietly as possible. When he reached the top of a small rise, he saw what must have been a 250-pound adult male hog digging in the ground. After removing his goggles, he took his time lining up the animal in the crosshairs of his night vision scope. He knew he'd only get one shot. He slowly let his breath out, held it, and pulled the trigger. The hog jumped as the bullet entered its right shoulder. It shrieked, stumbled once, and took off running.

Noah knew these hogs were one of the toughest animals to kill, but he was surprised the hog hadn't gone down. He scrambled to his feet and began jogging after the animal. But as he passed the spot where the hog was digging, he stopped dead in his tracks.

"Sweet mother of Jesus," he whispered. A human arm protruded from the dirt at the bottom of the trough the hog had opened. He removed his cell phone and called the County Sheriff's office.

His call rang four times before the on-duty officer answered, "Colleton County Sheriff's office. Officer Mike Brown speaking."

His hand shook, and his breathing quickened. He tried hard not to drop the phone. "Mike, it's Noah Martin. I got a dead body here."

~~~~
~~~~

The Colleton County Sheriff's office was located in Waterboro—about six miles from Noah's farm. It was about forty-five minutes later, and the sun was up by the time Sheriff Seth Johansson made it out to the Martin farmhouse. Noah and Elizabeth were on the porch when Johansson arrived. Noah told his wife to stay put and met the sheriff when he got out of his patrol car.

Johansson removed his hat and nodded to Elizabeth Martin before acknowledging her husband. "Morning, Noah. Officer Brown tells me you found more than you bargained for this morning. Tell me what we got here."

Noah began explaining what had happened when two more county police cars arrived at the farmhouse. Sheriff Johansson instructed his officers to contact Doc Wilson, the county coroner. After Noah gave Johansson a quick recap of what had happened earlier that morning, the two rode Noah's ATV as far as they could, and they walked the rest of the way to where he'd shot the hog. There was no mistaking when they got close to where he'd found the body—the smell was overpowering.

A hanky covered Noah's nose and mouth as he approached the hole. The sheriff stopped him. "Hold it right there, Noah. This here's a crime scene."

"Sorry, Seth." Noah pointed to the dug-up area. "Seth, I hit that hog dead-center and stared after him when I almost tripped over this. I swear I just about crapped my pants when I saw that arm sticking up. It was almost like it was pointing at me. Still got the willies."

Johansson used his cell to take several pictures from various angles before putting on elastic gloves and approaching the body. He bent down for a closer look at the arm. It was bloated.

"How long you think it's been here?" Noah asked.

"Hard to tell. Our forensics boys will give me some idea once we get the body dug up and back to the county lab. Let's get back to your place. I want my officers out here to tape off the area and make sure it stays secure until the body is removed."

ABOUT THE AUTHOR

Geoff Collins holds graduate degrees in business and finance and a master's degree in education. He has held multiple management positions in Fortune 500 companies and was CEO of a Midwest advertising and public relations firm.

After a successful career in business, he taught elementary school for fifteen years. His passion for teaching reading and writing to his students led to a career as an author of both children stories and adult mysteries.

Geoff lives on Johns Island, South Carolina, with his wife, Sally. He has three grown children, Max, Leigh, and KC, and four grandchildren, John, Collin, Cora, and Lily.

OTHER BOOKS BY
GEOFF AND ART COLLINS

Nikki and the Tree Keeper

"What a wonderful and lovely tale!"

"Nikki is a heart-warming and inspirational story of finding your place in the world."

"Nikki and the Tree Keeper is magical."

"The illustrations are beautiful and add so much to the book."

www.booksbycollins.com

The Christmas Token

"The Christmas Token is a heart-warming holiday tale about generosity, memories, and family."

"The artwork in this tender story is superior!"

"The Christmas Token should become a family tradition to read as the Christmas season begins!"

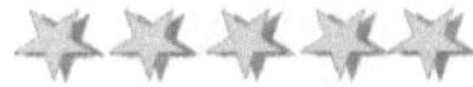

"Excellent!"

"Lovely book! My kids have read it many times over the holidays."

www.booksbycollins.com

The Adventures of ...
Archibald & Jockabeb

"One of a kind!"

This is the best book EVER!!!!!! Dragons, Indians, horses, evil crows, there is nothing like it! I loved it ... can't wait for more adventures to come.

"A majestic tale—Harry Potter meets *The Indian in the Cupboard*"

Loved reading these books. I quickly got hooked, dug in, and engaged with the characters. Wonderful stories.

"Rich in vocabulary!"

This book is rich in vocabulary. I can't wait to read all the other Archibald and Jockabeb books!

"Best of the best!"

In the Forest is an outstanding book! The characters are great and help make the wonderful story come together.

"Terrific series of action books!"

www.booksbycollins.com

White Cloud and the Golden Canyon

Excellent Native American tale for children and adults alike.

Wonderful life lessons for all.

Very enjoyable and true to our culture. (Akta Lakota Museum)

www.booksbycollins.com

The Black Creek Mysteries

Alex Foster and Travis Sanders live in a small southern Ohio farm town named Rivers Edge. Their first adventure takes them to the remote desert town of Sunshine, Arizona, where they find themselves in the middle of the Legend of the Apache Death Cave. The following summer, after Alex and Travis graduate from high school, they head to the small fishing town of Black Creek, Maine, for a relaxing vacation before they both head off to college. Their trip becomes anything but relaxing when they discover a mysterious creature in an underwater cave and a network of deadly gunrunners.

www.booksbycollins.com

The Mercy Killings

"Well Written … Interesting Characters and Plenty of Suspense"

Good mystery with interesting characters and plenty of suspense. A cybersecurity expert is hired to determine if narcotics theft is taking place at Charleston SC hospital and who is behind it. Well written with lots of fascinating details.

"Wonderfully Crafted Story Set in Charleston"

Wonderfully crafted story set in Charleston, SC—great story line and vivid imagery. Collins follows Giordano with insight and honesty. Can't wait for Nick's next adventure.

"A Fast and Exciting Read"

The book was a fast read. It was exciting and held my interest throughout. Hope to see more from this author.

www.booksbycollins.com

The Tools of the Trade

Mario Rossini's Jersey syndicate, the Beltran-Lyve Cartel, and the KKK's Confederate White Knights are all battling for control over Charleston's drug trade. Nick Giordano and his friends once again find themselves entangled in the fight. And this time they may all be targets for the legendary Mafia hitman, Carlos Tucci.

"Another Wild Ride"

Tools of the Trade takes us on another wild ride with Nick Giordano and his crew. Collins, as he did with his previous book in this three-part series (volume three is coming in 2019), deftly weaves on intricate story line that builds to a satisfying, thrilling end. Highly recommend Collins, a writer who deserves a vast readership.

"Excitement and Suspense"

Excitement and suspense as mafia and white supremacists fight over the drug market in Charleston SC. Characters well-developed and interesting story line.

www.booksbycollins.com

Shark Bait

Nick Giordano and his friends are drawn into the dark and dangerous world of the Russian mafia. The East Coast Russian mafia boss, Dimitri "The Shark" Pavlov, and his enforcer, Viktor Dudko, are using Charleston's Port Authority terminals for drug smuggling and human trafficking.

"Hopefully More to Come"

In this series, which sadly wraps here with Book Three, Collins found a higher gear with each, serving up a fresh batch of nasty folks for the series' core characters to root out and take down. That the books were set in Charleston only added to their delight. The only rotten aspect here is that this is the last we'll see of Nick Giordano and his pals—that is, unless, this crew comes around for cameos in one of Collins' future works. Hats off!

www.booksbycollins.com

A Death in the Family

Detective Adam Stone and his partner, Marcus Williams, are part of Charleston's elite Organized Crime Unit investigating a spike in the city's heroin and fentanyl drug trade. During a raid of a major drug distribution house, the shot-caller of the Bloods is shot and killed by Adam. Shortly after that, his wife, Ann, is found murdered. Initially, the Bloods are the obvious suspects. However, as the story unfolds, several other women are murdered, and the list of possible suspects grows. It soon becomes apparent that there is a serial killer roaming the street of Charleston.

www.booksbycollins.com

Prime Suspects

Prime Suspects is the second in the Adam Stone action-packed murder/mystery series. The dead body of the Joe Wallace, one of Charleston's premier defense attorneys, has just washed up on the shores of the Ashley River. Wallace possessed a dubious reputation as a heavy drinker, gambler, and frequent user of various controlled substances—not to mention his notoriety for chasing skirt. There are no shortage of suspects, and as Adam Stone moves deeper into the investigation, the list continues to grow. One by one, he eliminates the potential killers until he finds himself face to face with the most dangerous of them all … the prime suspect.

www.booksbycollins.com

The Sandman

In the third book of the Adam Stone detective series, Adam and his partner, Marcus Williams, investigate the late-night murder of a Charleston physical therapist. Soon two other therapists are murdered, and the detectives find themselves embroiled in the middle of an international Chinese opioid smuggling operation. The case eventually leads to the discovery of a connection between the Chinese Triad and the Chicago mafia. The possibility of additional murders rise as word on the street hints that an old mysterious mafia hitman has arrived in Charleston. Adam and Marcus know that they will now come face to face with the legend of the one of the world's most deadly assassin—the Sandman.

www.booksbycollins.com

Reading Partners is a nonprofit literacy organization that recruits and trains community volunteers to provide one-on-one reading tutoring to students in under-resourced schools across the country. This highly effective program has helped thousands of children master the fundamental reading skills they need to succeed in school and beyond. For more information, please visit www.readingpartners.org.

"Literacy is not a luxury; it is a right and a responsibility. If our world is to meet the challenges of the twenty-first century we must harness the energy and creativity of all our citizens."
—President Bill Clinton

www.ingramcontent.com/pod-product-compliance
Lightning Source LLC
Chambersburg PA
CBHW021313190726
48288CB00003B/828